BEYOND MIDNIGHT

For Dona,
Leave a couple extra
lights on when you read
these!

by S.R. Dixon

BEYOND MIDNIGHT

by S.R. Dixon

All rights reserved under International and Pan-American Copyright Conventions. Published in the United States of America by Ozment's House of Twilight Press.

Previously published stories:
"Caged Blonde Foxes," *City Slab*, issue #5, Fall 2004
"Chilling," *Night Terrors*, issue #8, Fall 1999
"Leave 'Em Laughing," *Black Petals*, issue #51, Summer 2010
"Ohtohway," *Night Terrors*, issue #14, Fall 2005.

This is a work of fiction. All characters and events portrayed in the stories contained herein are either products of the author's imagination or are used fictitiously.

Cover illustration, book design, layout, and typography by Benjamin Gorman.

978-0-9829721-0-6

Book manufactured and bound in the United States of America.
Published October 1, 2010, in Lanesboro, Minnesota.

Special Thanks

For the awesome look of the book as a whole, I give total credit and grateful thanks to the artistic eyes of Ben Gorman, Stef Dickens, and Adrienne Sweeney. Thanks to my readers—Gabe, Stan, and Tim—who helped me to tell the difference between the stories in my head and the ones I'd actually written down. And I would be spinning my wheels in a great big mudpatch of nowhere without my editor, Nick Ozment, who kept pushing up to the last minute to make each story the best that it could be.

Most special thanks to my #1 fan—Stela—who's helped me every step of the way putting this collection together and inspired me to see this project all the way through by telling people about it when I was too shy to. All my love to you and Twinkles.

Table of Contents

Introdcution   ix

Ohtohway   1

Midnight   15

Caged Blonde Foxes   29

Simple Simon   41

Chilling   55

Miss Cavern Queen   69

Leave 'em Laughing   103

Rapture   113

Straw Man   127

Back of the Closet   141

introduction

Lemme tell you about the scarecrow. My first vivid impression of him, I was just a little tyke…

Step on a crack, break your mother's back. I was the last of the Cub Scout pack that evening, waiting restlessly in the Den Mom's living room. My own mother was running late. Just enough time for me to pick up a children's picture book off the floor and start flipping through it.

Inside was a spooky little story about a boy walking home late one evening along the cornfields. And the scarecrow starts following him.

It wasn't a nice Wizard of Oz scarecrow. No. It was the Bogeyman.

Scarecrow, you were the scariest thing I'd ever seen. I recognized you: you were the thing in my worst nightmares, the horrible ones that a boy would do almost anything to forget.

I sat there wondering if Mom would ever come. And worse, wondering if it would matter. Mom might not be able to keep me away from the scarecrow. Not even Dad. Fear—not the heart-racing kind, but a sort of melancholy, a pensive awareness—settled over me. Nor did it help that I think I had a touch of fever that night.

That night, staring at that storybook (which undoubtedly was not intended to be even half as frightening as it was for me in that particular mood, at that perfect receptive moment), I think that was when it first sunk in that I would die. Knowing not just in an abstract sense, but realizing that someday this will end. The curtain will be drawn back, and I will be thrust into the Unknown. Maybe even tonight, the thought slithered across my feverish young brain. And will the scarecrow be there waiting for me?

Adults stop fearing the Bogeyman, right? Ask yourself that again, the next time you're alone in an empty, echoing house, and you hear a noise. Or the next time you're walking along a deserted street through a forest of shadows. Creeping around behind and beneath more prosaic terrors—sickness, loss, crime, financial ruin—is this fear of the Unknown. Of what lies just beyond midnight.

Poe knew it well. Just re-read "The Masque of the Red Death" for the perfect blueprint of the Bogeyman. While everyone is going about their lives, having a ball, there is one at the masquerade for whom the grotesque mask conceals something far worse. And that clock in the black-and-blood-red room is ticking inevitably toward midnight, when the ineffable truth behind the mask will be revealed.

H.P. Lovecraft knew it well. "The oldest and strongest emotion of mankind is fear," he once wrote, "and the oldest and strongest kind of fear is fear of the unknown." There is a reason why he is the greatest writer of the uncanny or horror tale of the twentieth century, as Poe was of the nineteenth. In the best of his tales, one gets glimpses of the scarecrow—often a cosmic scarecrow, that comes from dimensions beyond human comprehension. Always stalking us, even when we have pushed him far, far into the back of our minds for a while.

Which brings us to Scott Dixon, and this collection of chilling tales. Scott is a Poe scholar, and a student of Poe and Lovecraft. Scott wants to scare the bejeezus out of you. He wants to unsettle you, to get under your skin. To get you to hear, just for a moment, the ticking of that clock. As any horror fan knows, it is a delicious thrill, this intentional inducement of gooseflesh, this purposeful attempt to get the hairs to stand up on the backs of our necks. A bit of inoculation, perhaps? Like going on one of those amusement park rides that simulates the experience of free-fall without our having to jump off a cliff. Maybe. Whatever the reason, some of us just feel the need to periodically get back in touch with those childhood night terrors.

The characters in these stories are, for the most part, everyday people. People like you and me. Only, they come face to face with the bogeyman.

That sound in the closet? Scott opens the door and makes us look. That deserted road we're walking down, trying to reassure ourselves

we're all alone? He taps on our shoulder and points back to that silhouette coming just up the path in the twilight, that has been dogging us,
slowly but relentlessly, lurching along on creaking legs. Time and again,
he re-introduces us to the scarecrow. It comes in different guises, under
different names. Mr. Sliver. The Stranger. The Straw Man. But they're
all incarnations of that scarecrow. That's where I know him from. My
thanks to Scott for renewing the acquaintance.

— Nicholas Ozment
September 10, 2010

Ohtohway

The first time she noticed the bird, Beth was staring out the window of the restaurant. Jason sat opposite her, finishing off the fast-food hamburger and fries she'd only picked at. She felt queasy, and didn't want him to see it on her face so she looked across the icy parking lot. The cars scurried in and out underneath low, gray clouds. Each one looked the same as hers—streaked white from tires to door from the rock salt spread across the roads.

Her gaze passed over to the gas station across the way to see if it had a car wash. A small lighted billboard for Mrs. Underwood's Antiques stood nearby. Located downtown another mile-and-a-half down the road. A large crow perched on top, holding on with long, thick talons. It sat so still, Beth wasn't sure at first if it was real. It had the most enthralling eyes. They sparkled like crystal, and even from a distance, she thought she could tell they were focused on her. In fact, the longer they stared at one another the larger its eyes grew, as if trying to take her all in. A cramp stabbed her in the stomach and although it was impossible this soon, she thought she felt the tiny heartbeat in her belly start to skip and run.

Jason touched her hand. "Hello? Planet Earth calling."

Beth's attention snapped back to the table. "What?"

"I said, 'Ready to go?'"

Beth stared back silently for a moment. Jason's face took a while to come into focus, as if she were seeing him through a clouded lens. "Sure," she finally answered. "Do you want me to keep driving?"

Jason grinned. "No, I think I'd better take over." He reached out for the keys. "Are you okay?"

She nodded, and leaned forward to accept a peck on the lips. Outside, the wind's chill began to dig in as the couple crossed the parking lot. Beth absently buttoned up her jacket. Eight more hours until they reached her parents' house. Eight more hours of trying to find the right words, but not really wanting to. Sometimes she wondered if he already knew. Other people did. Other women. Mothers. Beth could tell by the way they looked at her.

She waited for Jason to get in and unlock the passenger door for her. Out of the corner of her eye, she noticed the billboard again. A second bird had joined the first, and now both were following her with their eyes as if they could see down into her body. Beth shivered under their stare—scavengers looking her over as if she were something on the side of the road.

They didn't blink. They didn't look away. Beth hurried into the car and locked the door.

A strange sensation roused her from a light sleep. Beth sensed the sideways motion of the car, and jolted herself fully awake. The rear end was starting to fishtail. Jason wrestled with the steering wheel as the car went into a gentle spin. She gripped the sides of her seat. The falling snow reflected the headlights back into her eyes. Every muscle tensed and locked.

Slowly the car came to a stop—roughly facing the same direction as before with all four tires still on the road. Beth sat frozen in place until Jason forced a half-hearted laugh. "Well, that was more exciting than it needed to be."

"What happened?"

He shrugged. "We started to slide, that's all." He pressed lightly on the accelerator and the car began creeping forward.

Beth pulled her coat back over her lap. She folded her hands over her tummy, then in a flash of self-consciousness, let them drop to her side. "Well, don't go so fast."

"I'm not."

"I mean it. How fast are you going right now?"

"I'm barely doing thirty. We're all right."

Jason leaned forward and snapped on the radio. A burst of static screamed from the speakers. He quickly turned the volume down, and began feeling around behind him in the back seat. Beth kept her attention glued to the road. She thought she felt the car start to slip again.

"Jason…"

He brought both hands back to the wheel. "See if you can find a CD for me, Sweetie. I need to listen to some music."

Beth twisted around to fish in the darkness and clutter of the back seat. "I think we should just pull over."

"Sure. Would you like the gully on the left or the right?"

"I'm serious."

"There isn't any place to pull over. It wouldn't make sense to wait it out anyway. The roads will just get worse."

Beth's fingertips brushed the nylon CD case. She grabbed it and pulled a disc from one of the middle pages without looking and inserted it into the player. A gentle jazz piano and saxophone duet came on over the speakers.

"I want to stop at the next town and get a motel room."

Jason exhaled loudly through his mouth, blowing a drooping bang temporarily up and off his forehead. "I'm okay. I can keep driving."

"It's not worth it. We'll call my dad and tell him we'll be there in the afternoon. It's not like we're going to make it when we'd planned to anyway."

"Then let me know if you see something. I'm not gonna go driving around back roads in this mess."

"I will."

Beth settled back into her seat. The car felt as if it had shrunk in half and she desperately hoped to see a rest stop or gas station up ahead where she could get out and breathe fresh air. There was nothing. The snow had started falling shortly after they got back on the interstate after dinner. It was an early storm for the season, but a brutal one. After passing through Erie, they heard on the radio that Buffalo had been completely shut down, so they turned off onto a local route which then dwindled to a winding country road. The storm seemed to follow, picking up every time they thought it was tapering off. The highway was under several inches and there hadn't been any other traffic since leaving the interstate, not even a snowplow. All she could see were trees, their snowy branches weaving a barrier along their route. At times they loomed ahead until the road curved away, seemingly at the last minute.

A gust of wind buffeted the car from the side. Beth shivered although the heater was going full blast. Dozens of different thoughts ran through her head, each one competing for the opportunity to be given voice. Yet whenever she opened her mouth, she closed it right up again. None of the words felt quite right when they came up to the tip of her tongue. And when she thought about it, did she have to say anything at all? Babies were not in the plan for either of them. She could handle the operation by herself. Jason wouldn't even need to know.

Beth rubbed her eyes. They were tired and starting to burn. What if Jason did want the baby? She tried to imagine what it would look like, and she couldn't. What if looking at the baby was like looking at Jason? Sometimes she didn't recognize him even up close, and she couldn't remember how she had gotten to this place in her life with this particular man. Even worse were the moments when she suspected that everything else was correct, and she was the stranger walking through another person's life.

Beth leaned her head against the window. The trilling of the air vents sounded like a purr. Her eyes opened and closed in long, heavy blinks until all at once she was asleep again and dreaming that she was floating through a clear, night sky. The air felt cool against her face. All was still until she heard a soft, pattering beat—like rainfall on canvas. Beth put her hands on her belly. A warm pulse awoke deep within and began to spread across her body.

She looked around. A flock of birds had appeared. They soared with her, long wings beating slowly. The tiny heartbeat started to pound faster. A new sound filled the air—a murmuring voice. Beth strained to hear.

The birds suddenly stopped their flapping. Their eyes seemed to probe under her flesh. Beaks as sharp as knives pointed in her direction.

They attacked.

Beth snapped awake with a yell.

"Jesus!" Jason said. He turned to look at her. "You okay?"

Beth nodded. She started to speak just as a dark shape swooped across the front of the car. Jason cried out and jerked the wheel, sending the car into a violent spin. The whole world seemed to fall silent. Beth couldn't hear the music, or the wind, or the screeching tires. The moment was frozen in anticipation. She turned to look at her husband. The whites of his eyes glowed in the orange light from the dashboard.

She sensed the emptiness a split-second before it took them. Suddenly, they were no longer on the road but bouncing backwards down a sharp slope. She shut her eyes and braced herself. Every thump made her heart leap and sink in the same instant.

The left rear wheel rolled over something that served as a ramp. Jason's side lifted in the air just before the car slammed to a stop. The impact threw Beth into the air, and the safety belt yanked her down again. The seat back broke and slumped off its joints.

For several seconds—each of which passed like an hour—all Beth could hear was her own panting. She gingerly turned to look at Jason. His head was slumped forward into the cushion of his air bag.

"Jason?"

He moaned. Beth reached over to lay her hand on his shoulder. He leaned back, grimacing.

"Are you all right?" she asked.

"Feels like I wrenched my neck real good. How 'bout you?"

Beth nodded even as spikes of pain ran across her lower back. Jason reached up to turn on the dome light. "Oh God," he said looking at her. "You're bleeding."

He pointed at Beth's forehead. She touched the spot with her fingers and felt the wetness. Tears welled in her eyes, and she squeezed them shut which set her head to throbbing. She heard a zipper opening, and then something cottony was pressed into her hand.

"Here, put this on your head."

Beth opened her eyes. Jason had given her a white sock from his overnight bag. She dabbed at the wound at first, then applied the sock with pressure. Tiny stars momentarily filled her field of vision. Jason unbuckled his seat belt and opened the door. A gust of icy wind blasted into the car.

"Where are you going?"

"I'm gonna take a look." The car door made an awful screeching noise as Jason swung it shut. Beth tried to find a comfortable position in her seat. The snow was starting to freeze and now it spattered against the windshield. Up in one corner, she noticed the glass was cracked in a spider-web design centered around what must've been the point of impact for her head.

Movement across the hood of the car caught her attention. A crow walked along the edge, all the way from the driver's to the passenger's side. When it finished its cross, it stopped, turned, and looked back at her.

Her door swung open. Beth yelped.

"Easy, easy." Jason knelt in the snow, huffing from the cold. He touched her hand—she grabbed his and squeezed. Half-laughing and half-crying, she fell into the embrace he offered.

"Oh my God," he whispered in her ear. "Are you all right?"

"I'm fine. I think it's stopped bleeding already."

"That was so stupid. I just got spooked when that damn bird flew right across the road."

"A bird?" Beth looked out at the hood of the car. The crow was gone.

"I saw a light at the bottom of the hill. I think it's a house." Jason looked at her closely. "Can you walk okay? We should go and use their phone."

Beth wobbled a little as she got to her feet. She looked up towards the highway and couldn't see it. The size of the hill and the angle of the incline made her heart clutch in her chest.

The wind drove needles of cold under her skin as she bundled herself in her jacket. Jason started to guide her down the hill, and at first she couldn't see much in that direction. But once they worked their way around a cluster of trees, she could see a weak, yellowish light. She kept a grip on Jason's hand as he made a beeline towards it. The snow was up to her knees, hiding large stones, stumps, and logs. Every misstep brought a stabbing complaint from her lower back.

Close to the bottom, Beth tugged at Jason to make him stop. She put her hands on her knees to catch her breath. Her body felt cold all over except where she could feel a warmth, like a candle's flame, glowing in a tiny niche in her belly. She tried to will the heat through the rest of her body.

Beth straightened up and strained to listen. Between gulps of air, a rustling sound had reached her ears.

"Ready?" Jason asked.

"Sh!"

Beth turned around. A few yards behind them, shadows fluttered amongst the trees. She held her breath. Crows. There were a dozen she could see, but many more by the sound of them. They hopped across the snow, flapping their wings. Several of the larger ones seemed to keep an expectant gaze on the couple.

Jason took her hand again, and Beth was only too happy to follow. Just ahead, the woods opened up to a vast field. In one corner, about fifty yards away, stood an old, one-story cabin. The logs were caked with snow, with icicles hanging like daggers under the eaves. A floodlight nestled under the peak of the roof illuminated the front. As the couple drew near, the light popped and went out. Beth nearly jumped into Jason's arms. He laughed and patted her on the back.

"God, I hope someone's home."

Jason pointed to a pale blue light flickering in the front windows. "There's someone here. Or they left the TV on. C'mon."

Beth glanced back over her shoulder. The whistle of the wind and the rustling, scraping noises coming from the trees gave her a chill that had nothing to do with the cold. She hurried after her husband and nearly bumped into him on the doorstep.

Jason pounded on the door twice, waiting a moment in between to listen. He put his hand on the knob while glancing back at Beth. It turned easily.

"Don't!" Beth grabbed at his sleeve.

"Oh, don't freak out. The least they can do is let us in. It's freezing out here."

Jason pushed the door open. A glacial wind blasted the couple, followed by a frosty mist that engulfed the doorway. Beth's chest tightened, and for an instant she thought to turn and run. Then she remembered the birds, and it was as if she could feel their collective gaze crawling over her now. She stepped up and went inside.

As she passed through the curtain of fog, Beth felt as if she were inhaling pure cold. She hastened her way through the mist and stood just inside the cabin. The interior was one enormous room. In a far corner, a frost-covered wooden table was tipped over on its side next to a stack of matching chairs. A layer of ice two or three feet thick covered the walls. The room was lit by a bluish glow that came from a sculpture of ice shaped like flames and set into a fireplace. The light made her skin tingle where it touched her face.

Beth's heart clenched in and out of a tight fist. The walls were covered with carvings of birds, sparkling under the blue firelight. It gave them a sense of flight—slicing like razors across the sky. She thought of her dream, and the flock that surrounded her.

Jason grabbed her arm and pointed. "Look."

Standing next to the fireplace was the body of an old woman, frozen into the wall like a bas-relief. Her flesh was grayish-white, stretched across little more than bone. The body seemed too frail to support even the shriveled head, which hid in shadow from every angle.

Jason swore under his breath. "How long do you think she's been here to get like that?"

All Beth could do was look at the woman's face. Something made her believe the eyes were frozen open, fixed in an eternal stare. Behind those eyes, Beth could see barren fields under a deep carpet of dead-white snow. Thick clouds hung low, blocking all but the bleakest light. Trees and bushes were sheathed in ice, their branches cracking in the wind. Beth wrapped her arms around herself, shivering violently.

"Are you all right?" Jason asked.

"Cold," was all she could say. Her voice sounded like it was coming from a mile away. She felt as if she were sliding across the fields. In the span of a heartbeat, she hurtled past acres of desolation conquered by winter. Up ahead appeared the cabin, and then all at once Beth was looking inside—looking at herself staring into the oncoming rush. She tried to pull back at the moment of collision, and felt her feet slip out from beneath her. The world tumbled upside-down and sparks of blue light burst all around her. Something smacked her in the back of the head. And then there was darkness.

Beth lay on a hospital bed holding her swollen belly. A dozen or so crows watched from their perches on white crystal walls which stretched up to a bright blue sky. Every now and then, she would meet the gaze of one, and it would open its beak and call to her. The words were so quiet, it was hard to tell if she heard them with her ears or from within her own mind.

oh-toh-way, *they seemed to say, over and over. And each time she heard it, a burning chill ran through her body.*

A swift kick from inside her belly made Beth jump in surprise. She ran her hands all over her ballooning tummy, playing follow-the-leader with the pokes and prods. Warmth spread through her and laughter pealed in her ears. Her heartbeat and her baby's played a duet she could feel as well as hear.

Shadows flashed over her face. Birds circled overhead once…twice… before swooping down, one after the other, covering the floor and then standing on top of one another until they were stacked higher than the walls. And they kept coming. The flock filled the room, blocking the sun and plunging everything into darkness. The only thing Beth could see were shining eyes burrowing their gaze deep into her belly. She felt the baby squirm and twist. A thousand whispers, like prayers, filled her ears: oh-toh-way…oh-toh-way…oh-toh-way…

She awoke to an electric tingling in her belly. Beth rolled over on top of Jason's coat, which was laid out on the cabin floor. A dim and flickering light made long shadows dance across her legs. At first she thought it was the ice sculpture, but then she realized the light was coming from a low fire burning in the corner next to her. Nearby, Jason was breaking up a frost-covered chair. He had it on its side, and was jumping down on the legs to snap them off.

She tried to sit up. Stiff muscles rebelled, making her suck in a breath through clenched teeth. Jason jumped at the sound, and he whirled about.

"You're awake. Are you okay?"

As Beth shook her head gently, Jason knelt beside her with a chair leg in one hand. "You had a bad fall. Knocked yourself out."

Beth's eyes widened. "How long?"

"Long time." Jason pushed up his glove to look at his watch. "I was a little worried. You were talking in your sleep."

"I was?"

Jason reached back to stoke the fire. "Just mumbling, really. You said the same word a couple of times. Sounded like 'Ottawa' or something."

oh-toh-way, Beth thought. Flapping shadows filled her mind's eye.

"I don't remember."

Jason stooped to blow on the coals. They flared briefly into flame, but just as quickly dropped back into a weak glow. Beth crawled closer until warmth touched her cheeks. She put one hand against her tummy, trying to massage it beneath her coat. The tiny pulse pumped her own blood in and out, trying its best to chase away the chill. She closed her eyes for just a moment. The face of the old woman flashed before her.

oh-toh-way...

Her eyes flew open. The room felt like it tipped suddenly to one side. Beth leaned against the wall, using it to help her stand. She looked back at the ice sculpture. The light from Jason's fire made it hard to tell for certain, but she could swear the blue ice flames were blazing more brightly than before. It seemed to be reaching out. A tingling, pins-and-needles sensation ran through her belly. Jason looked back over his shoulder and caught her wincing.

"Are you sure everything's okay?"

Beth saw him mouth the words, but his voice was muffled. The room seemed to be filled with whispers. "I don't know," she said.

Jason came over and put his arm around her. "It's almost dawn. I was on my way back to the road to flag down a snowplow or something."

Her eyes widened. "I'm coming with you."

"I don't know if that's a good idea. You can stay here by the fire."

Beth stared at Jason. His face had never looked more blurry than now, and she grabbed onto him as if to keep from slipping further away. When she spoke, her words seemed to fall into a chasm between them. "Take me with you," she tried to say.

Jason wrapped an arm around her and they headed for the door. Rays from the frozen fire fell on Beth, and as they did the tingles became tiny stabs. The light started to have a rhythm, different from the random flicker of flame. It picked up a beat, the same as the rapid pattering in her belly. Beth used all her strength to turn her back on it and keep moving.

They finally reached the door, and Jason pulled it open. The storm was over and night was beginning to give way to dawn. A perfect blanket of snow glowed like a fantasy landscape, burying their tracks from before. Beth waded into the snow up to her thighs. The cold instantly bit into her, but she forced herself to move forward.

As the couple approached the edge of the woods, Beth started to make out movement in the trees. Dark shapes hopped from branch to branch, circled in the air, and swooped down to the forest floor. They started yammering excitedly as Beth came closer—a thunderous cacophony in the stillness. Jason tugged at her, but she let her hand drop out of his as the crows came out of the woods, walking across the top of the snow. One giant bird stepped ahead of the rest. It was almost as tall as Beth's waist and wore a coat of feathers darker than midnight. She stared, transfixed, at the streaks of color passing through the bird's eyes. It stood tall, spread its wings and flared its feathers. Beth's heart pounded in her ears.

The crow opened its long, sharp beak.

oh-toh-way… oh-toh-way…

A wave of terror washed through Beth. She reached out to pull Jason back, but he had already stepped forward, waving his arms and shouting. The flock parted, moving off to either side, but then closed their ranks behind him. The large crow turned its head to look back at Beth, and its eyes rooted her to the spot. She could read a fervor in the way they twinkled and danced.

She instinctively crossed her arms over her belly. Jason was moving further and further away, but she couldn't call to him. Only one word would come to her lips.

oh-toh-way… oh-toh-way…

Jason stopped. He looked around at the crows surrounding him. A ripple passed through the flock as they all turned to face him.

His eyes met Beth's. "Sweetie?"

The flock burst into flight. All at once a wall of slashing beaks and talons sprung up between the couple, and the air filled with screams. Beth ducked low and spun around. The only clear path remaining was back the way she had come, and she practically swam through the snow to get back to the cabin door. The doorstep tripped her up, and sent her sprawling to the floor.

"Beth!"

The sound of her name made her turn. Jason had fought his way to within a few feet of the cabin. His face looked as if he'd been peeled. Beth started back for him, but a twisting sensation filled her belly. She stopped. Her heart, and her child's, hammered in time together. Jason stretched out a hand for her. The glove had been ripped into tatters, and the skin was drenched with blood. As she watched, a crow landed on his shoulder, gouged him to the bone, and flapped off again.

The flock descended upon Jason and he disappeared from view. He was still calling for her, but his cries became fainter under the screeches and caws. A sob broke open in her chest, but when Beth opened her mouth to scream, no sound would come out. She backed away from the door on her hands and knees, unable to look away.

The birds dispersed. Nothing was left on the snow but bloodstains. The flock had taken Jason away.

Beth retreated all the way into the far corner. A few crows landed just inside the cabin door. They seemed to inspect the room as they entered, taking in the carvings and the ice sculpture. From Jason's fire, she grabbed the unlit end of a smoldering chair leg and brandished it like a baseball bat. Several of the birds lifted their wings and pressed in on her. Beth took a swing at them, making the embers on the end of her makeshift club glow. The flock continued to advance until Beth felt her back hit the wall. From the hearth, the frozen fire blazed as brightly as the sun.

Cold tears stung her cheeks. She slid down the wall and huddled in the corner as if she could make herself disappear into the shadows. The crows did not approach any closer, but stopped and watched. She tried not to return their stares, but everywhere she looked she was greeted with shiny black marble eyes and a whisper that echoed in her mind.

oh-toh-way… oh-toh-way…

Beth opened her eyes. She wasn't aware of having drifted off to sleep, but a blue sky was visible beyond the icy window panes. The thought passed briefly through her mind that the plows would certainly be on the roads now, just like Jason had said. But she couldn't move. Her legs were numb, and a layer of frost covered her from head to foot. She actually felt warm, but it was a liquid sensation that seemed to be flowing out of her, like water down a drain.

The crows paid her little attention as they milled about the cabin. The frozen fire reached out with a fierce, steady light that grew brighter as it touched each bird. Their shadows stretched across the room to join together on the far wall to become the silhouette of an old woman with a hooked nose and jaw, spindly legs and spiky hair like a crest on top of her head.

The flock murmured amongst themselves at a cracking sound emanating from within the frozen fire. Beth dropped her eyes so she didn't have to see. On the ice between her outstretched legs was a single word written with the charcoal end of the chair leg still leaning against her shoulder. There, she had traced the letters over and over again.

Ohtohway.

The pattering heartbeat in her belly started to skip, even as the last matchstick's worth of warmth bled out. A burst of light exploded from within the fireplace, and then it went out. The birds fell silent. Beth looked over and could see that the flock had backed away from the fireplace, crowding themselves into the far corners of the cabin. All eyes fixed on the old woman's body.

A noise like breaking glass filled the room. The old woman turned her head. Beth called her by name.

Midnight

*O*netwothreefourfivesixseveneightnineteneleven—MIDNIGHT!
As he ran past the gas station where county road 12 arrived in downtown Scanlan, a stabbing pain crept up the side of Noah's ribs. *Mile and a half,* he thought, trying to ignore the sensation of a sewing needle working in and out of his skin. It seemed further, and he immediately pushed that thought out of his mind. Bad enough to have to run on such a sweltering night. Thick, humid air clung to his skin and filled his mouth with more moisture than oxygen. It was a night he should have stayed home, cranked up the air-conditioner, and watched a B-movie on cable TV. But he'd felt itchy. Anxious. He didn't want to be alone. That was nothing new, but tonight the feeling was so deeply rooted that he wondered if the loneliness might have been planted there.

Could it work that way? Noah wondered. The Run had been a part of his life since childhood, and yet so much was still a mystery. All he really understood was the price of losing.

Regardless, he'd picked tonight to go out, without any specific destination or anyone in particular to look for. Of the three bars in town, the one that jostled his senses the least was Snoose's at the far end of downtown. It was doing modest business when he'd walked in an hour ago. Noah nodded at the regulars while he got his beer and wound his way to the patio out back. Unoccupied at the time, which suited him.

He was a loner, not so much by choice but by fate. His closest friends were the dead ones.

Toes up, knees up, he coached himself as he ran by Scanlan Foods. Two more blocks to get past the pizza place, and the hardware store, and the feed store. His hometown was one where you could throw rocks down the middle of the main street after nine p.m. and not hit a single thing. The only visible activity tonight came from the American Legion, where a respectable karaoke version of "Long Cool Woman" spilled out through the open door. But otherwise, Scanlan was a town where the sidewalks rolled up at sundown, even in the summertime. There wasn't much to do except hit one of the bars or, if you were underage, wander down by the old railroad tracks and find a place along the river to get high or laid—or both.

Noah once thought about moving away. Most of his friends did once they finished high school—or at least tried to. They headed for big cities and bigger opportunities. It was one conversation topic that he and Tracy often came around to while they lay side by side in bed in his dorm room, waiting to sink into sleep. It was like a fork in the road of their futures, waiting for them up around the bend. They had grown up together, been initiated into the Run together, and yet she was never going to go back to Scanlan after college. He couldn't imagine being anywhere else. He knew the roads here like the hallways of his own house—how the short-cuts connected, where the sharp inclines and the fast tracks could be found. When it was time to Run, he didn't want surprises.

onetwothreefour…

In the window of the quilt shop at the edge of downtown ("Stella's Stitchin' Time"), he spotted dark shapes, wispy like a morning mist, flying down the sidewalk just behind him. Tracy. And there was Paul, and Tracy's brother Alan, too. Twenty-nine, nineteen, and nine years old respectively. It was always the four of them on the Run, although tonight Noah couldn't tell if they were racing with him or against him. Either way, it wasn't supposed to matter. Coach Irwin used to tell his team, *Never look behind*. A good runner has to feel the others without seeing them—and Noah could do that. On the oval tracks of his youth, he could sense the other runners, and even what it was motivating them. School pride, family pride, personal pride.

Deep in the ghost-eyes of his friends tonight, he felt their hate. It burrowed into his skin like a rot, then spread quickly because there was a sour place in his own soul where he hated himself too. For running. For escaping.

For living.

In an alley off to his left, something moved in the shadows. Could've been a dog, or a straggler from the Legion, but Noah didn't think so. The image summoned in his mind's eye was that of a man—tall and thin like a sapling, wearing the night draped over his shoulders. He had bone-white skin, with long fingers like garden snakes hissing and darting as he grabbed at the air where Noah had been an instant before. Thirty years ago, Tracy had been the first to see this man slipping out of the darkness as if it had parted for him—the star of the show making his entrance through the curtain. She once told Noah her theory that this sliver of a man waited in the night—always there—hiding in plain sight like one of those optical illusions. Invisible until you looked in just the right direction from just the right angle at just the right moment.

But when you saw him once, you could never not see him again.

Noah used to think of him as the thin man. It was Tracy who first called him Mr. Sliver.

Her class ring bounced outside the neck of his polo shirt. Noah tucked it back in as he turned the corner onto Water Street. *Easy... easy...* His pace felt good and his breathing had gotten deeper, easing the stitch that'd grabbed him when he'd first taken off. Fortunately, Snoose's back patio hadn't drawn a crowd and so only a few other people had been there when he sensed the soft tear of the night. What must they have thought—to see him leap down the steps of the patio and sprint away? *Too fast*, he thought, *too soon*. He knew better than to do that. He ran track in school, even got a scholarship to the U, and nowadays signed up for every charity 10 and 25K he could find. But it was all really an excuse for more training. Around town, he freelanced for a couple of different contractors and hired out to local farms for field work April through November. It kept him lean. He was a few weeks shy of his fortieth birthday and could still run close to a seven-minute mile.

Fast enough for tonight? He didn't know. The Run had never been against Mr. Sliver alone before.

twothreefourfive…

The night of the First Run had been much like this one—the kind of wet, swampy heat that drags everyone into a stupor except insects and children. Four friends played in Alan's backyard—a square clearing bordered by the house, two strips of trees, and then deeper woods straight out the back. Thousands of cicadas sang in the lingering summer twilight, and it had just begun to grow genuinely dark when the play changed to hide-and-seek. Alan, Noah, Tracy, and Tracy's twin brother, Paul.

While Alan counted, the rest of them headed for the woods where the trees cast the heaviest shadows. Noah picked a healthy-sized pine close to the lawn to crouch behind. As the children entered the woods, the tree-song had fallen quiet, and Noah could not bring himself to venture any deeper into the dark silence behind him. It enveloped him, and made his own heavy breathing thunder in his ears. He tried to hush himself and found that he couldn't, which made him feel easy to find, and that made his heart and lungs pump even louder.

He heard Alan crashing through the brush nearby and thought about bolting, but strangely, his galloping heart would not let him move. He was frozen on a summer night, and could only hope to get tagged just to bring the game to an end. The air had turned thick, and the night itself seemed to creep across his face. He needed to move. He needed to stand, tagged or not, and race towards the warm light of the porch, into the open air of the backyard. He was going to do it. Now. His legs wouldn't obey. *Now!* he screamed inside his head. *Now, now, now—!*

A shriek—a real one—broke the unbearable silence. *Tracy*, Noah thought. Actually, it was Paul. He bolted like a deer through the trees. It broke the spell, and suddenly Noah erupted from his hiding spot too. The sudden freedom blew all his fears away. They were children at play, and the game was all. Running for "home" (the black walnut at the end of the driveway) before "It" (in this case, Alan) caught them, or the first kid "home" could count from one to midnight and cancel the tree's immunity for anyone who wasn't already there. Paul was the fastest of them all, but Noah and Tracy were closing the gap quickly. Alan followed right behind.

In the nightmares that followed, Noah could see the tree about twenty yards away. Paul's hand, like his, was stretching for the trunk across a moment frozen in time. *Almost... almost...* Then suddenly, Tracy's screams knifed through his ears, snapping him back into his own body. Noah looked at her, and then to where she was pointing, and in that instant his blood turned to ice. Even Mr. Sliver, standing by the walnut tree, looked surprised—as if he also had been caught in the game. Then, his black eyes glittered like diamonds of night. White hands wrapped around Paul's arms, lifting the boy so quickly that his feet were still paddling in mid-air.

MIDNIGHT!

Everyone took off running, each in their own direction. Noah heard Paul's screams chasing him down the street and trying to slow him down. He didn't look back. He ran until he thought he was flying all five blocks back to his house. He exploded through his front door and might've run straight out the back again if his dad hadn't practically tackled him in the kitchen. He had no voice to say what he'd seen, and it seemed like forever before his heart no longer felt like it was going to burst out of his chest.

None of them ever actually saw Paul's body. No one was allowed. When the teachers were far enough away not to hear, the rumor-mill at school churned out gory details of what Paul's folks had found when they ran outside to see what the screaming was about. Their son's head was intact. The rest of him was in scraps—like he'd been run through a paper-shredder. Ribbons of flesh, intestines, and muscle stretched like taffy across an eight-foot smear on the grass. They had to use a rake and shovels to gather his remains.

The town decided it had been a cougar attack. Such a thing was practically unheard of, but not entirely impossible in a small town in the Minnesota Northwoods. Friendly counselors with placid eyes and smiles told Noah any other memory came from shock—a young mind processing terror as best it could. After a time, he almost came to believe that himself.

threefourfivesix...

A new twinge on the outside of his right knee began to set in as Noah turned the corner at Ichabod Street and started up Church Hill. All he had to do was make it up this side and down the other to get "Home"—a pre-fab job he rented from one of the families whose farm he worked on. But his first few strides uphill made him feel as if he'd come to a stop. All his momentum seemed to vanish and panic swept through him. *On your toes*, he coached himself. *Swing the arms out.* Tracy's ring weighed him down like an anchor. The hill might have been a mistake. Shorter, yes, than going all the way up Water Street and cutting over by the school. But faster? He feared not.

No, no! Too much thinking. He had to make his thoughts light to keep his feet light. Like the First Run. That one was easy because it was instinctive. Monster appears—child runs. Nothing about that needed questioning or considering. But hardly any experience can be that innocent twice. The second time, even if it comes as a surprise, is stained with awareness.

The Second Run happened the night before Alan's nineteenth birthday, right at the start of fall break. He and Alan drove home together from the U, and after dropping off laundry at home, headed for a campsite tucked in the back corner of a campground/RV park owned by Alan's aunt and uncle. It was mid-October—the tourists had left and the hunters wouldn't arrive for another few weeks. Friends and family would gather to celebrate tomorrow, but this was the night-before-the-party party. Just them two guys... and Tracy. Alan had felt like calling her up at the last minute and Noah certainly didn't object.

They raided the nearby woods and empty sites for dry brush and split wood left behind, and soon a nice fire had them all feeling warm. It was either that, or the bourbon. Or the company. Noah watched Tracy secretly as she laughed, chiming in with her own occasional rude comment. Her face glowed in the firelight. Where most of the coeds he knew showed only questions in their eyes (if anything at all), Tracy's had a clarity and a connection to something beyond herself. It made her look like an actual adult, instead of a tall child-thing with breasts. She was beautiful in a way beyond her skin, or her hair, or her face.

At some point in the midst of the joking and the storytelling, Tracy grew quiet. It seemed like she was taking on the thousand-yard stare that comes when the drinking buzz turns the corner into inebriation. But Noah realized that she wasn't staring at nothing. She was watching.

More than that. Reaching out with all her senses for… something.

While still looking out into the night, she reached over and took Noah's hand in hers. Suddenly it didn't matter that they weren't alone. A yawning emptiness opened in his chest that only this woman was going to fill. He could already feel how warm and soft she would be in his arms, and not holding her right then and there made him lonelier than he'd ever been before. He turned to Tracy, hoping to see her eyes looking for his. And they were—thrown wide open in panic.

"Go, go!" she yelled.

He didn't think—he obeyed. They were both on their feet at nearly the same instant as Noah caught a glimpse of long, white fingers stretching out from the flickering shadows between the trees. His imagination filled in the rest—how a slit had opened in the shadows. Long arms followed the fingers, then the shoulder, then the head. A dark glee danced in Mr. Sliver's eyes, like a child's upon seeing an array of presents laid out beneath the Christmas tree.

Noah didn't know where he was going—he was just following Tracy and trusting her instincts. And that left room for a frightening thought to surface. Alan was now up and running too, and in a fair race, Noah had never once finished ahead of his best friend. In high school, and now at university, they placed first and second at every meet and every practice. But this time, Noah had the head start. *Never look behind,* Coach said. And Noah didn't want to. As long as he didn't fall off his pace, his head start was just large enough to hold up.

The old joke was like a slow, jagged rip across his heart. *I don't have to outrun the bear—I just have to outrun you.*

And so Noah kept his eyes looking nowhere but full-front. He didn't see what happened, but he heard it. One moment his ears were full of his own panting, his feet slapping against the cracked and buckled driveway of the campground. Then Noah heard Alan cry out. Once. It was a little sound, no more than a sudden, almost accidental, whimper. Noah had made the sound many times himself when seeing another runner pass him on the inside track, or in the very moment of feeling his foot turn awkwardly just before going sprawling to the ground.

"Help," Alan said.

no, dude, don't ask me to turn around, i can't turn around—

But the next sounds were the ones that haunted Noah. They burrowed into his memory—waiting, like ghosts, for the empty hours of the night to wander from one dark corner of his mind to another. Alan's screams were glass-shattering. Defenseless wails in the face of terror and suffering, utterly stripped of any consciousness or self-awareness. Purely primal screeching.

Then silence.

Even after catching Tracy, and reaching the safety of the lodge where Alan's aunt and uncle lived, Noah couldn't keep still. But neither could he lead the police back toward Alan's body. There was only one direction his legs would allow him to go, and so all he could do was point the way for brave rescuers more blessedly unaware than he of the creatures of the night. When they returned, however, Noah could smell the blood and gore on them—like dogs who roll in rotting corpses in the woods. The men shivered as if they'd never feel warm again, and they too gathered like Noah in the furthest corner of the room away from the door.

Tracy, however, was the very definition of stillness. Once seated on the sofa, she never stirred. Only her eyes moved, scanning the bustle of sheriffs, troopers and EMTs with a vibrancy exactly the opposite of her unremarkable expression. Noah watched people speak soothingly to her and then discuss shock among themselves as if she wasn't registering anything happening around her. However, Noah could tell she was taking in absolutely everything on a level of understanding impossible to describe.

While his own adrenaline and shock were still flooding his system, having her nearby made him feel safer. She was a sentry. A watchdog with electronic ears and infrared eyes.

fourfivesixseven…

By the time he reached the top of Church Hill, Noah's chest was sore from the pounding of his heart. His lungs squeezed precious air in and out like a set of creaky bellows. Somehow he had not felt long fingers circle around him, or steely arms lift him into a mouth as wide and sharp as a shark's. Was he winning? Or was it because of the two buildings—St Luke's and Grace Lutheran—facing one another on opposite sides of the street? Grace was where Alan's service had been held. Another funeral, another closed casket. Noah and the other pallbearers lifted it easily to and from the hearse, almost as if it had been empty. There was simply not much recovered to bury—not after another rare, yet vicious cougar attack.

Tracy stayed at Noah's side for weeks afterward, utterly silent in front of other people and only mostly so when they were alone. Neither one of them could stand to be separated from each other, and yet being together felt cruel. Being with Tracy made Noah feel alive, and being alive made him feel dirty somehow. Soured.

Help, Alan said, in the dead of the night.

By the end of their rawest grieving, it could be said they were "going together." It lasted a year, and while they slept together every night, only once did it involve sex. On that night, she overloaded him with her taste and her touch. Being with her, the way she took him inside of her, felt like a forgiveness he couldn't grasp for himself. He joyfully drowned in her embrace for an hour of love-making, but the next morning their relationship returned to how it'd been before. She needed to be near him, and have him near her, but bristled at actually being touched.

One night, while January winds blew down from the north and froze the condensation on his dorm's old windows, Noah awoke suddenly. Tracy was sitting in his rickety wooden desk chair, a blanket over her shoulders like a cloak. She was staring out the window, seeing without seeing. Once his eyes could make out the expression on her face, he sat up in alarm.

"Is it here?"

"No," Tracy said. "Shh, shh."

"How do you know?" Noah asked.

"I'm not sure." She turned in her seat to look at him, and her eyes seemed darker than the gloom, like twin pockets of night's deepest shadow. "But he will come again."

"He?"

"I used to draw him," she said with a heavy breath. "Without even thinking of him. My mom once asked who that was in all my pictures. I told her his name was Mr. Sliver because he was tall and slender like the thumbnail of the moon."

"What is he?" Noah whispered. "Why is he after us?"

Tracy shook her head slowly. "Maybe he comes when he's strong enough to cross through the night. Or bored enough. I think he's always near, but we actually saw him because…" She shrugged. "I don't know. But now we have to run. That's all we're here for now—to be in the Run."

A week later, she told him she was leaving school and transferring to a different one out of state starting next fall. It was never mentioned if he should follow, and somehow he knew that she didn't want him to. Tracy meticulously reclaimed all the stray belongings she'd ever left in his dorm room—books, t-shirts, notes and letters, even pens and pencils. Everything but her class ring, left on the top of the old apple crate Noah used for a nightstand. There was no note to go along with it, but he understood they were not meant to speak or see each other again.

At least, not until the next Run.

fivesixseveneight…

The pain in his knee now felt like a knife stuck all the way from the outside through the inside of his leg. He tried not to give in to it, but a definite hop had come into his stride. *Keep it short*, he reminded himself. *Short and even. Strike the middle of the foot.*

After Tracy left him, whole years seemed to pass in a single turn of the clock. He graduated from university, worked a few different jobs. His father passed away, and then his mother soon after. And the most important thing in his life was always The Run. He trained for it. He meditated, and read a bookcase full of New Age titles about auras. Jogging along the back country roads, he was (or imagined he was) aware of invisible legions in the woods and prairie grasses surrounding him—birds, squirrels, rabbits, snakes. Their energies shifted around him and sometimes he thought his eyes must look the way Tracy's had looked that night around the campfire.

He wanted to be ready. He needed to be ready—to fight Tracy for that split-second head start. Of all the memories he had of her, that one ached the most. She'd saved his life. Alan had been sitting just as near, but she didn't choose him. Noah thought that meant he was special, but he didn't know how. And when she chose him again, for a lover, he thought that was going to be the moment when he would realize what was special about himself. But it hadn't happened then either.

Maybe, he thought, that was the reason she had to leave. Although, she wasn't really gone. Not in his mind. When he closed his eyes, every woman he dreamt about had her face. In any crowd, he was sure to hear her voice or see the curve of her cheek out the corner of his eye.

And then one day—*almost ten years ago*, Noah thought, while trying to ignore the pins-and-needles sensation filling his feet—he felt like a trip down to Minneapolis to spend some time in the big city. The January thaw had begun, and a day of rain had melted the snowbanks by a few inches. As soon as the sun went down, the temps would fall back below freezing, but for now people coming out of work didn't burrow into their scarves and collars and scurry to their cars. They strolled, breathing deeply of a bracing air that refreshed rather than punished.

Noah walked a bike path, a half-mile loop around one of the smaller lakes downtown. The evening sky was deepening from azure to black, the snow banks catching the last glow of daylight and casting a bluish light on the scene. He passed a few couples enjoying a walk together. A small crowd was at the other end of the lake skating under the light of the streetlamps. They laughed, crashing into each other, stumbling across the uneven surface.

He wasn't watching where he was going and stepped directly into the path of another walker circling the lake in the opposite direction. Noah apologized instantly and found himself looking into a pair of green eyes he'd seen every night in a decade's worth of dreams.

The wintry blush on Tracy's cheeks went pale. "Sorry," was all she said before whirling around and running full speed back the way she'd come. Noah didn't hesitate either. He started off, immediately feeling the weight of his boots like stones on his feet. Somewhere close behind him, he sensed the night rip and part.

Mr. Sliver was here.

Once again, Tracy's senses and her reflexes gave her an advantage out of the blocks. Noah bore down, focusing for the moment just on matching her stride. The cold seemed to steal his breath and made his chest feel close to bursting. He managed to pull alongside Tracy, just off her shoulder. With another burst of speed he could pull ahead, but his body didn't—or couldn't—respond. Too much weight in the bulk of his jacket, not enough air in his lungs. And then, memories began to overcome his senses—the warmth of her body, the smell of her hair while resting her head on his shoulder, the glow of her secret smile meant for only him to see.

Tracy glanced back. For a moment, their eyes met and shared a haunted look. Something started to drag on him. He was feeling caught in molasses, his arms and legs slowing while she pulled clearly ahead. A chill raced through Noah. Electric tingles ran through his flesh in anticipation of how Mr. Sliver's fingers would feel slicing into him—through skin, and muscle, and bone.

Suddenly, it was Tracy who screamed. As if in slow-motion, Noah watched her plant her outside leg on a patch of black ice and suddenly wrench sideways. She twisted almost completely around and crashed into a snowbank. Before he could even process what had happened, time suddenly skipped forward and he zoomed five yards further down the path. She screamed his name.

Don't look back.

He ran. Still he ran, until the searing pain in his chest and his ribs could mask the agony within. He came full circle around the path and blended in with the back of the crowd that had gathered. His gasping went unnoticed amidst the crying and screaming of those with a closer view of Tracy's body. Someone sounded like they got sick at the sight—twice—and suddenly the police were there. A pair of uniformed officers ushered the crowd a hundred feet away, and when they came to Noah to ask what had happened, he hid his mouth with his gloves to hold in the mad outburst dancing on his tongue. "Cougar attack," he almost told them.

He read about her funeral in the newspaper, but didn't go. Instead, he drove to a Target store and spent forty minutes picking out a silver chain. Sitting in his car in the parking lot, he put Tracy's class ring on the chain, the chain around his neck, and wept while sleet lashed at the windows all around him.

Help me, Tracy said, in the dead of the night.

one, two, three, four—

As Noah took the corner on to his home block, one foot slid a little on pine needles at the side of the road. But he didn't let that break his stride. His house was a few hundred feet away now. His right leg now screamed every time his foot hit the pavement. *Knees up, knees up!* A soft breeze picked up behind him, giving him a bit of tailwind. *Good, good.* He needed the help. The sweat made his shirt feel a whole pound heavier. Everything felt heavier now—his arms, his legs, even the air.

five, six, seven—

Four houses to pass until his. Now three. Noah's lips pulled back into a toothy snarl. His feet felt hot. Final sprint now—time to find something more to give. In his neighbor's darkened picture window, he spotted them again. Alan's angry eyes, Paul's silent curse. He squeezed his eyes closed before he could see any more. Not Tracy, he thought. Sweat stung his eyes and made them tear as he cut across his front lawn. *I loved you, I loved you, I did—*

eight, nine—

The tailwind suddenly gusted, as if it would pick him up and hurl him to the finish.

ten, eleven—

With a cry, Noah hurled himself up the steps—

MIDNIGHT!

He crashed against his door, clinging to it to hold himself up. Noah wanted to cry, he wanted to laugh, but all he could really do was breathe—and that was like inhaling needles. A car drove down the street one block over. From somewhere, a dog barked.

Noah stared at his yard. It was empty.

I beat you, he wanted to shout, but his breath hitched, then caught in his chest. The weight in his chest melted and the release was an even greater agony. Loss, guilt, grief—they all flowed through him. With a tinge of victory. In the midst of it all, he felt light. And alive.

"I beat you," he whispered. Not by chance, or a lucky break. By running. Just by running.

The door opened behind Noah, spilling him backwards across the threshold. A moon-white face with dark, glittering eyes leaned over him, filling his vision like the full moon. Mr. Sliver reached out one long finger. It slithered under the chain around Noah's neck, lifting it so that Tracy's ring caught the light from the streetlamps. The creature's lips cracked open, showing off black, knife-like teeth in a smile.

"You just might've," it said, "without this."

Caged Blonde Foxes

Zanna flipped aside the ragged backstage curtain, leaving the cavernous emptiness of the main room behind her. It was worse than hunting season. She was on her fifth shift in three days and there hadn't been more than a dozen men in the club at any one time. And even they only stared into their drinks, or at the table tops, or straight ahead at nothing at all. Their eyes were either glassy and blank, or else wildly shifting from side to side, scanning the shadows, not resting on any one thing for long. Certainly they weren't looking at her. She got more attention from the poles than she did from the boys.

Zanna dropped into her dressing room chair and pulled a tattered cotton bathrobe over her shoulders. Goosepimples ran across her skin. The weather was turning cold early, and she wasn't ready. Icy winds off Lake Erie had chased summer quickly away, and brought in steel-grey clouds to hang over the city. Fewer and fewer people appeared on the streets, and those who did hurried on their way. It was even that way at the mall. For the first twenty minutes, she had thought she was the only one there. Half the stores were empty, either locked up behind a steel security web, or simply standing open, as if waiting for someone to come along and flip the lights. At O'Dea's Department Store, the racks closest to the entrance showed signs of having been rifled through, but no one had touched any of the dresses or coats sitting in the shadows.

Surely there was nothing in there, but somehow it just seemed safer not to venture into the darkness.

It was the quiet that disturbed her most. The bustle of traffic using the freeway ramps near her apartment building had dwindled and then virtually stopped. All along the street, empty windows greeted her, watching her every step. Because of the abandoned cars, she had to park down the street from the front door and walk half a block. In the silence, she could hear the wind slicing through the streets. She jumped every time it caught a can and sent it clattering across the pavement, or the violent flapping of a plastic bag caught in a tree branch. The shadows moved, if only in her mind. She may as well be at work, then, with the music and the lights and the boys.

The lights outlining her mirror started to take the edge off the chill in her breasts. She leaned forward into their warmth, cradling her head in her hands. In the mirror, she glimpsed Allison's long legs striding for the door.

"It's like a church service out there, Birdie."

The other dancer flipped her off without missing a step. *You're sagging*, Zanna noticed playfully. She could tell. She was used to recognizing the way skin bunched in places and hung tiredly in others. Her cellulite creams had their own drawer in her bathroom at home. Every lingering look was like getting half the bill, and so Zanna let them look until she knew they were ready to pop their shorts. If any guy left the club with cash still in his wallet, it wasn't for a lack of trying.

C'mon baby. A whisper floated up from the back of her mind. *It'll feel good.*

"Is it really bad out there?"

Zanna turned and looked over her shoulder. An apple-cheeked girl named Cheryl sat in the furthest corner of the room, with her back nestled protectively against the walls. She was already in costume for the next set—blonde wig with a maroon bikini top and g-string. It was almost painful for Zanna to watch her cradling a fluffy, wire-reinforced "tail" in her lap like a kitten.

"'Cause if it's dead it ain't worth it. We'll get like, what? Not even fifty?"

"We get what we get." Zanna pumped lotion from a flowery dispenser into her palms and rubbed under her arms and across her chest. She caught a glance at herself in the mirror. More sunshine, that's what she needed. Maybe a trip to her cousin's place in South Carolina. She puffed out her cheeks, pulled at the pale skin and massaged it between her fingers.

"Maybe we shouldn't bother." Cheryl's eyes darted back and forth between Zanna and the door.

"Fine," Zanna blurted. She rubbed her face with an old washcloth, feeling it scratch her in a comfortable, familiar way. "You tell Treves."

"He ain't even here. Lots of the boys are out 'cause of…," Cheryl snapped her gum, "well, you know."

"That shit's far away from here."

"Nuh-uh. My brother's in the Guard and he said last weekend they was gonna set up on 90 and 77 and 71. To keep out the deadheads."

Zanna picked up a foam wedge and dabbed fresh concealer over her freckles and spots. It brought a little color back. Cheryl kept on talking, even if it was just to herself. "I mean, like, where is everybody? If nothin' was happening, they'd still come. So maybe we just skip it tonight. Zanna? Whaddaya think?"

Zanna tried to block out the thoughts Cheryl was putting into her head. She'd heard the stories—that people were disobeying the cremation laws, that the cops couldn't find all the homeless and the overdosed junkies in time. But it wasn't like you saw the deadheads just walking through the Flats. The real trouble was down in farm country, like Stark or Wayne County. Just the other day there was the news report about state troopers following a bloody path of horse carcasses to a whole Mennonite community being held hostage. It was bad down there, the news said. Almost as bad as in the beginning.

"Even Treves ain't—"

"So what?" Zanna snapped. "He'd know. All those girls who ain't here, what do you think is going to happen to them? If you ain't here, then you ain't working and if you ain't working then you ain't gettin' paid." She kicked the wall and shut herself up.

The outer curtain suddenly parted to reveal a hulking young man in a black t-shirt. The club's logo, in neon green, stretched across his barrel-sized chest. "Birdie's dying out there. Got to get you in the cage."

"Karl?" Cheryl sat straight up in her seat with her best schoolgirl pout on her lips. "Don't leave us out there too long if nothin' goin' on."

Karl rolled his eyes for Zanna's sake, then stepped back out. Zanna reached for a gym bag under her chair and pulled open the zipper on one of the outer pockets. She fished out a plastic baggie half-full of flat, aspirin-like tablets. She popped one and dry-swallowed while throwing on a wig and bikini outfit identical to Cheryl's.

Allison suddenly burst into the dressing room. She had maybe three bills clenched in her hand.

"Fuck!" She threw a towel against the far wall.

Cheryl vacated her corner, fastening the wire tail to her g-string. Zanna followed her out to an iron, circular staircase all the way in the rear of the backstage area. Electric tingles crackled like sparklers in her head. She stopped to let Cheryl go up the stairs first and her eyes lingered over the hitch and jiggle of the younger girl's ass. She followed it all the way up to the top and along a catwalk running out over the main floor. Karl waited for them by a converted diver's cage, set to hang teasingly over the v.i.p. tables. He held the door open for the girls like a concierge.

Cheryl nervously entered the cage while Zanna stopped to lift her top. "Tit check."

Karl cupped one breast in each hand, squeezing them like melons. "Feelin' ripe, feelin' juicy."

She winked at him before readjusting her outfit. Then, she stepped rudely inside the cage, making it swing. Cheryl instinctively clutched the bars until it stopped. Karl closed the door behind them and made his way to the winch controls.

Zanna stole a peek at the tables below. They were practically empty. She sighed and silently wondered what she had expected. Birdie should be working the room, selling passes to the front. But nobody was here, not even the regulars—guys who were in the club on Christmas, Easter and Mother's Day. A nauseous heaviness settled in Zanna's stomach and threatened to pull her down out of her high.

"Gentlemen!" Karl's deep voice boomed from the speakers. "The Venus Cabaret, Home of Cleveland's Heavenly Bodies, presents the wildest two-girl act in the city. Here's Holly and Pamela, Caged Blonde Foxes!"

Thunderous techno music exploded through the club. The winch creaked and lowered the cage into a storm of flashing yellow, red and green lights. Zanna and Cheryl grabbed the bars to swing and grind. They rubbed their bodies against each other, slipped off the bikini tops and let their fingers and tongues run all over each other.

No one was watching.

Zanna circled back around Cheryl, bent the younger girl over, and went to work fondling her breasts and rubbing her pelvis against Cheryl's ass. Cheryl sank slowly to her knees, then sat up against the bars with her legs dangling over the empty tables. Some guy got up from his seat and headed for the bar, passing almost directly below the cage without so much as a glance upwards. Zanna buried daggers in his back with her eyes. She knelt down and started stroking Cheryl under her g-string. Cheryl started moaning, making the great orgasm-face and licking her lips. Zanna looked out across the club, hoping to catch Karl's attention and give him the signal to haul their asses out of there. All she could see was Allison going from table to table trying to get someone to at least talk to her.

Her thoughts drifted. The music was new. She listened for a while. It was mixed badly, like some garage band's demo disc. The lead singer sounded a little like the Rude Man. He had been a junior, she was a freshman. He had an old ratty couch at his parents' house where his band practiced.

C'mon, baby, he whispered in her ear, *I'm so full.*

Suddenly Zanna snapped out of her reverie. Someone was shouting—the words drowned out by the music. She let go of Cheryl and shielded her eyes with her hands, trying to see through the glare. People were moving to the door at the back of the club and there was more yelling. The hairs on the back of her neck stood on end. She spotted

Karl moving toward the crowd, thick arms pumping in his kick-ass stride. She yelled to him; he was too far away to hear.

And then an unmistakable shriek sliced through the din. The crowd that had been streaming toward the exit were suddenly swept back as if by a great wave. Snapping and crashing sounds rose in volume to compete with the music. Zanna looked frantically for Karl. Another sharp scream filled her ears, and suddenly Allison broke into view, racing toward the cage. A shambling mass of shadows trailed close behind. She made a running jump to get on top of one of the tables and from there leapt for the cage. It pitched wildly, knocking Zanna backwards on her ass. Allison clutched at the bars. trying to pull herself up. Dark blood flowed freely from a nasty wound across her forehead.

The dark shapes stepped into the flashing lights. Rainbow colors illuminated the jagged ends of mud-smeared bone poking out through shredded strips of clothing, muscle and skin. Some had the flesh peeled back from their faces, revealing the grinning, drooling skull underneath. In an instant, they yanked Allison down into their midst. Bloody, grimy mouths pulled the flesh from her bones.

Cheryl screeched right into Zanna's ear. Now the things were reaching up for the tasty legs dangling outside the bars of the cage. Zanna leapt to her feet. She wrapped her arms around Cheryl's chest and heaved, but one creature grabbed hold of her ankle and greedily sank its teeth into the meat it held in its hands. Cheryl howled. She lashed out with her other foot, smacking the zombie repeatedly in the side of the head. It finally let go, and Zanna threw herself backwards to haul Cheryl out of reach. The creatures hissed and moaned, clawing at the empty air.

Zanna laid Cheryl down on the floor of the cage. The zombie had ripped away a chunk the size of a tennis ball from the back of her shin, biting through muscle and tendon. Zanna grabbed the discarded bikini tops and wrapped the wound as tightly as she could. She looked around for Karl—for anyone. The club was totally overrun. Besides the things below the cage, there was another clump by the door, scavenging for scraps. And others were making their way into the back areas: the dressing room, the storeroom, Treves' office. Her head spun. It wasn't possible. There were patrols to pick off the deadheads, and the National Guard, too.

"Cheryl?" Zanna prayed there was still some lucidity in the girl's eyes. They were tear-filled and glassy. Zanna hauled off and slapped her. "Cheryl! Your brother! Where was he gonna be?"

Cheryl stared back blankly, mouth hanging open. Zanna hit her again. "Goddamnit, listen to me! Do they know all these things are in the city?"

There was no response, except for fresh rivers of tears and mascara staining Cheryl's cheeks.

They'll know, Zanna told herself. She leaned back against the bars. Under the music, soft moans and hisses filled her ears. She dared to look down once, and all she could see were hands—stained with gore—reaching up for her. A cry bubbled up from within, but by the time it reached her lips, it was a mad giggle. She kept her mouth closed, and prayed silently.

Zanna's pounding heart snapped her awake. It was dark, but she could feel a powerful hunger, like a presence in the room. A thick, foul stench was in the air—a rotting smell that made her gag. Cheryl lay like dead weight across her lap. Her eyes darted frantically from side to side as they slowly adjusted to the gloom. The power must've gone out. The only lights came from the exit signs and stairwell floods, revealing eerie white and orange shadows moving below. Three figures stood directly below, gazing upward like children trying to catch snowflakes. Zanna's stomach twisted at the sight of their bloody faces, stained by the drippings from Cheryl's leg.

Her eyes burned—her contacts had dried out. She wouldn't have imagined being able to fall asleep, but then all of a sudden she was out and had no idea how long it had been. Long enough for her legs to have cramped up. Zanna shifted her weight. Cheryl stirred gently, but then her eyes flew open and she cringed as if to cry. No sound came out, just empty wheezing. Zanna squeezed and held her close for a moment.

Cheryl sat up and whimpered. "I can't feel it no more."

Zanna bent over the wound. It looked like a wet sponge, still dripping blood. But what concerned her more was the rest of Cheryl's leg. It felt puffy and swollen, and a mottled color had spread from the ankle all the way up to the thigh. A tight, squeezing sensation filled her chest.

Zanna looked overhead, trying to see if the catwalk was clear. The stairs were located far in the back, and maybe the deadheads were incapable of navigating the steep climb. It was at least a possibility.

I'm so full, baby, Rude Man moaned. *It hurts. I need you.*

"Hold onto the bars." Zanna picked up their bikini tops and started wrapping them around her hands.

"Where are you going?"

She pointed. "To the winch."

"No!" Cheryl sat up quickly. "Don't leave me!"

"No one knows we're here. They won't think to look for us."

"My brother'll be here!" Cheryl sputtered. "He knows! He knows…"

Zanna forced her voice into a steady and even tone. "We can signal someone from the roof. They'll have patrols out looking for people in trouble. We'll get outta here and get your leg fixed."

Cheryl hugged her knees to her chest as Zanna flipped open the side door. She reached out for a handhold and stepped outside. The sound of shuffling footsteps from below echoed in her ears. She refused to look down. She swung one leg up, trying to catch her foot on one of the cage bars running about waist high.

She missed. Her grip on the steel bars slipped and something coarse brushed the bottom of her foot. The image of dark shapes closing in filled her mind's eye.

Zanna clutched the bars with all her strength and hauled herself back up out of reach. Her heart was pounding like a fist in her chest, and she waited just a moment to steel her nerves. She swung a little higher next time and got her foot up to where she could pull herself up to standing on the bar. Then from there, she clambered on top of the cage. Cheryl just stared when she flashed a thumbs-up sign.

Woven steel cable descended from the pulley in the upper lighting grid to a carabiner about four feet above the cage before splitting into three smaller cables attached to the roof in a triangle pattern. Zanna tightened the bikinis around her hands. She reached up over her head and grabbed the main cable. With a jump and a grunt she tucked her knees under and pulled herself up.

And again. She reached up with her bottom hand and lifted. Her arms trembled. She tried to focus on something else.

It ain't nothin'. Rude Man pressed his weight on top of her. *Nothing at all.*

Zanna ignored the burning sensation in her muscles. She pulled herself up another foot, and without pause, reached up and pulled again. The catwalk was tantalizingly close. It looked like she could get to it if the cage would swing a little…

As she raised her head to the level of the catwalk, Zanna caught sight of a pair of tattered leather dress shoes. Her eyes walked up the ripped slacks, earth-splattered blazer and moldy, yellowed collar right up to the shriveled, rotting gray-green face. The zombie's mouth hung agape, drooling a brackish, viscous liquid.

It stooped and lunged for her. Zanna screamed. Exhausted muscles gave up the fight and she fell. She hit the top of the cage in an awkward position, and bolts of pain knifed through her lower back. The cage tipped wildly, and Zanna clawed for a hold. Her fingers wrapped around one of the roof bars, and she just about felt each of her knuckles pop from the strain. But she held on.

Quickly, she scrambled back to the center. Zanna lay gasping for a long moment before she noticed the blood and a new razor-sharp pain coming from a gash where she'd caught her arm on the clip. As she lay staring up at the catwalk, more zombies emerged from the shadows. Some bent low and stretched for her, as if they were extending a helping hand. They were everywhere—like roaches. She flopped over onto her stomach.

Cheryl trembled directly below. Some of the blood from Zanna's arm had dripped onto her face. Her eyes were no longer dull but glassy and shining.

Zanna turned away. Every heartbeat felt like a shuddering blow and the sound of the throng above and below her pounded in her ears like surf. She laid her head down with no strength left to cry.

Rock and roll!

Zanna sat on the forest-green slip cover, feeling the hard edges of the couch's wood frame poke her back and bottom. Brett and his crew were downing Budweisers in the Rudermans' basement. Brett Ruderman was sweaty from practicing. His stringy, Ted Nugent hair was plastered across his forehead. She hadn't been able to take her eyes off him while they'd played. She'd danced in her seat, her breasts bobbing freely under her halter top.

When they were all done, and the other guys had packed up their gear and left, Brett came right over to talk to her. He was so shy! He actually asked first if he could kiss her. She was going to explode if he didn't.

The first time he slipped his tongue into her mouth, she jerked back in surprise. That made him laugh.

C'mon, baby. *He pulled her back to him, rubbing his pelvis against hers. Fireworks went off in her head. He eased her down on her back, laying his weight fully on top of her.* It ain't nothin'. Just relax. It'll feel good.

Her head was floating. The basement suddenly seemed so hazy, she was almost sure she was dreaming. She felt him everywhere—pushing his tongue into her mouth, sucking on her neck, gripping her ass and unbuttoning her shirt. His touch was warm and cold all at the same time. Her last moment of clarity came when he started undoing her shorts. She put her hands against his chest to push him away. I'm so full, baby, *he said.* It hurts. I need you.

And then, in the next instant, he was inside her—the two of them bucking wildly on the couch making the old springs scream. She closed her eyes, and when she opened them again, she looked up and studied the leering face pressing down close to hers. It was close to someone she recognized, but not quite. The skin was jaundiced and pulled taut against the skull. Crusted, scabbed sores covered his cheeks and forehead. He stank of something old and musty.

She kept right on humping him, whoever he was. He was so heavy on top of her, she thought she was going to fall through the floor. She winced at the colossal grip he had on her shoulders, and the sensation of a thick icicle being rammed into her over and over. She squeezed him with her thighs. His body felt mushy. It bulged like bad fruit. He was going to pop. He was going to drench her. He was going to—

Zanna awoke suddenly, a hot flush filling her cheeks. She was panting for breath and a horrible taste filled her mouth with every intake. The zombies were ominously still, but the hunger radiated from them like heat. She could practically hear them calling her name.

Looking down, she saw Cheryl curled in a ball in one corner. The flesh looked puffy and hung loosely off her bones. Zanna eased her way back into the cage and sidled alongside the young girl, rubbing Cheryl's arm and thigh in long, soothing strokes. The skin felt clammy.

Cheryl stirred weakly, turning her face up to Zanna. They pressed cheeks together, and the odor was monstrous. Zanna cuddled up even closer, and brushed her lips against Cheryl's ear as she whispered, "I'd love it if you could take my mind off all this."

She held her breath before they kissed, but couldn't entirely avoid a taste of the air inside Cheryl's mouth—humid and stinking of rot. Zanna guided the young girl's lips to her own breasts and tummy. She was aware of more zombies gathering below. She rolled Cheryl over onto her stomach and sat on her back, kneading her shoulders like dough. She grabbed hold of Cheryl's left arm and pulled it back, rubbing the upper, meaty part. There was a moment, even then, that she hesitated.

C'mon baby, c'mon. It ain't nothin'.

Zanna bent Cheryl's arm at the elbow and pushed the hand up towards the back of the neck. Cheryl's sighs of pleasure abruptly stopped. She squirmed—not fiercely, more like the flopping of a landed fish. She didn't even cry out much when her arm made a cracking noise. Her whole body just seized up.

The zombies pressed close together to watch. Zanna grabbed Cheryl's right arm and held it easily in place.

I'm so full, baby. I need you. C'mon…

Zanna bent low over Cheryl's right shoulder. She let her tongue hang out and licked from side to side.

"Zanna," Cheryl moaned, "no…"

Zanna put her whole mouth to Cheryl's neck and latched on with her teeth. The meat pulled away with sloppy ease. Cheryl barely twitched, except in her eyes. A wave of groans passed through the crowd as Zanna dangled the stringy meat between her lips. She tilted back to show off the workings of her throat. She almost couldn't do it, but she forced herself to swallow and returned instantly to the wound to suck on the pulpy muscle and tissue. The juices stained her face from cheek to cheek. She dipped and fed, sitting up straight now and then to show what she had in her mouth. The zombies moaned over and over again. She could almost hear their beckoning floating up to her ears.

C'mon, baby, c'mon.

Be with you boys in a minute, Zanna thought just before she bent low, bit and tore.

Simple Simon

It was almost perfect.

Holding the steering wheel with both hands, Simon could imagine open road in front of him. The wind blowing through the windows filled the car with the smell of blossoms. Julie was in the seat next to him. She was laughing, and as long as he could hear that sound, then he didn't miss the other cars and trucks, their horns trumpeting. Or the radio. People talking. *Too loud! Why are they so loud? It's just the two of them—Simon and Julie. The only ones on any road, anywhere. Alone, and together.*

The world began whirling, dancing just beyond his ability to bring it into focus. The wheel of Julie's car, the view of the street through the windshield. The barrel of the gun. Everyone shouting. Simon squeezed his eyes shut, but that made the voices even louder and they too started to spin. The sounds were trying to take him under and drown him. He filled his lungs and yowled. It pushed back the other noises a little bit out of his head and so he bellowed again—louder and louder until he could out-howl everything else.

Hands clutched at his clothes, pulling him out of the driver's seat. But the door wasn't open and Simon just kept banging into it. He yelled at the hands to stop grabbing. Another body pressed against his, and Simon curled into himself like the bugs in the basement laundry room. Suddenly the door gave way and he was tumbling to the street. His palms scraped against the pavement. Prickly pain danced like a little fire across his hands. He clutched a fistful of his hair and yanked. The sharp sensation cut one clear path through the madness around him. He pulled again. It was like jumping on a tornado and riding it down to a stop.

The noises became clearer.

"…out of…now!"

Not just noise. Voices.

"Swear to God…you can't…"

"…no, no, no!"

Two voices. The louder one—the deeper one—was a man he'd never heard before. Too loud. Simon didn't know what he'd done to make the man have to be so loud.

"I'm not leaving! It's for my friend!"

That was Julie. What was she saying? He was supposed to listen to Julie. At the Center, she was the one who said when it was time to stop for lunch and when it was time to go home. Sometimes she sat next to Simon and helped him figure out what to write on the social service papers. She was smart—his brother Alan said so. Listening to Julie was as important as listening to Momma. What was she saying?

"Please, stop! STOP!"

Simon opened his eyes. Julie was leaving him. She was chasing a blue car (*that looks like julie's blue car*, Simon thought, *i was sitting in julie's blue car with two hands on the wheel always two hands*). A man was in the front seat where Simon used to be. He drove around the empty cars in the street, and the boxes and the suitcases and the shopping cart on its side. He didn't slow down, and even went up on the sidewalk where he wasn't supposed to go and knocked over a mailbox. And he didn't stop, didn't even slow down.

As Julie ran all the way to the corner, the street stretched like a rubber band. If it snapped, the street would be broken and he'd be stuck on the wrong side from her. Simon screamed her name. She stopped, going down on her knees. He hurried to her in case she was going to get up again, but she stayed on the ground, both hands clamped over her chest like she was trying to hold something there.

It was a long way to run and he had to breathe in and out a lot before he could say anything.

"Are you okay?"

Julie held up one hand so he would stop and wait. She was gasping too, but not in the same way. Her lips were drawn back and her breath whistled through her teeth like the wind slicing between buildings. Simon tucked his chin and mouth under the collar of his sweatshirt. Even so, he could still taste oily salt lingering in the air. It was always there, but huffing like this through his nose and mouth was like taking a long drink of something that coated the inside of his mouth and throat. For weeks now, the city had been smelling like the dried-out tidal pools after the crabs and panfish have shriveled and baked in the sun. When the smell first started to fill the whole city, the people started to go—most toward the water. The others went as far away as they could. The city became quieter and quieter as the shouts and the traffic and the screams in the night all went away. And for a time after, their echoes still came out of the steel and the concrete the way that a sidewalk still feels warm even under a summer moon.

But now, even those ghosts had died, and the only sound left was the wind coming in and going out…and coming in…and going out…

"Julie, I want to go." Rain was coming, and the nighttime too, deepening the color of the sky from yellow to orange to a reddish-brown over the harbor. He couldn't remember the last time it'd been blue. Maybe Summer. Now it always looked like it was going to storm, even when there wasn't a cloud to be seen. It gave Simon a tight feeling in his chest, like when he would stand at the edge of the deep end of the pool at the Center, slowly creeping his toes closer and closer to the water. Feeling like something was about to happen and the whole world was just waiting. Watching. Holding its breath.

He stared at the tops of his sneakers. White, with orange stripes. Alan had just given them to him not long before he had to take Momma away. Best sneakers in the world.

"Julie?"

"I know," she said between gasps. "Help me up."

Simon held out his hand and pulled her up. She stood, but not all the way straight. One of her hands was still clasped to her chest, and she draped the other over his shoulder.

"Put your arm around my waist, Simon," she said. "Help me walk."

His eyes widened. "Are you okay?"

She shook her head. "We have to go back to your apartment. Right now, okay?"

Julie stumbled on her first step, but Simon caught her, wrapping both arms around her waist. A lock of hair spilled out from beneath her hood and brushed against his cheek. Scratchy, like straw. Sometimes, he remembered, the sunlight through the classroom windows at the Center made her hair look almost blond, and when she sat next to him, she smelled of peach and berries. But Julie kept her hood pulled up all the time now, even when she was inside. Momma had done that too, before Alan had to take her away. It was supposed to help Momma's skin—the air made it so dry that she left big white flakes behind when she rose from her bed or the sofa.

Simon and Julie walked down the middle of the street, keeping distance from the dark doorways and darker alleys. Alan said meeting a fishie was like meeting a strange dog. Some were going to be okay, but some were going to be wicked mean, and you just didn't know. Best to keep away. Don't make any sudden moves, but always be ready to run.

After two blocks, the lobby door to his apartment building came into sight. Julie still clenched her teeth while she walked, like she was smiling all the time but Simon didn't like the way her lips were pulled back. It caused deep grooves to appear in her face and cracked the dry patches of skin on her cheeks and around her eyes. As they approached the outer door, he fished his keychain out of his pocket, looking through the colored rings. "Green, green grass of home," Momma used to sing. He found the green key, put it in the lock, and turned. They slipped inside and Simon pulled the door closed instead of waiting for it to float shut on its own.

The inside air didn't smell a whole lot better, and was a lot stuffier as well. But being closed off also made it feel safer as they walked through the small lobby, headed for the stairwell just past the elevators. They didn't work any more. Everything stopped working about a week ago—the elevators, the TV, the lights in the bathroom. When things didn't work, Momma always said to talk to Mr. Riegler, but this time Simon didn't want to. He hadn't seen the manager since before Alan and Momma had left and, one time, walking by his door, Simon thought he heard something moving in Mr. Riegler's apartment. He went to knock, but stopped himself just in time. He knew it was impossible, but somehow he could just tell what was on the other side—Mr. Riegler and his pasty, white stomach pressed against the door, his mouth making wet sucking sounds as the breath went in and out faster and faster in excitement.

Simon and Julie climbed the stairs with Simon counting each door they passed until they came to the ninth one. Here they went halfway down the hall while he flipped through his keyring again (*yellow, yellow, kiss a fellow*). Once inside the apartment, Julie made her way to the couch and lay down right away without taking her coat or her boots or her hood off.

"Do you wanna go to Momma's room?" he asked.

She waved a hand at him. "Let me…here for a minute."

Simon waited, watching Julie search for a comfortable position on the couch. She wasn't breathing as heavily as before, which Simon thought was a good thing, but it wasn't normal either. Every now and then something seemed to get caught in her throat, and her eyes got real big. The skin flaps on either side of her neck pulsed and pumped until at last she took in a whole gulp of air.

Her dark eyes searched most of the room before finding him. They looked swollen, starting to bulge out of their sockets. And they used to be green (Simon was pretty sure they used to be green), but now looked a smoky black.

"Water?" she asked in a voice barely more than a whisper. Simon nodded and went in the kitchen. Some time before Alan had to take Momma away, his brother started filling every container he could find with water—milk jugs, soda bottles, ice cream pails. That was a lucky-good thing to do, Simon thought, because the faucets stopped working about the same time as the lights and the TV. One last bottle was left on the counter—a half-empty two-liter originally filled with root beer.

Simon brought it back to the living room and put it in Julie's hands. She tipped it towards her mouth, but most of it splashed all over her face.

"Careful, there's no more," he said. "No more."

Julie's mouth worked open and closed a few times, like she was trying to swallow a bubble. "The rest…was in the car?" she asked. Simon nodded.

"Okay, okay." She took in a couple of clean, easy breaths. "So tomorrow… we find a car." Her neck flaps fluttered. "Someone who left their keys before…before they…"

"Went to the water," Simon finished. One night, a fight in the bathroom woke him up. He jumped out of bed and ran in to see Momma in the bathtub, clawing at the air and making a scary choking sound while Alan ran the faucet and tried to keep her head under the water. He had long red scratches down his neck and arms where Momma's fingernails—yellowed and hardened—had gotten him. *I have to take Momma to the water*, Alan explained, wrapping a bedsheet around Momma to pin her arms to her side. Even so, she thrashed so much that Simon had to hold all the doors open while his brother carried her all the way down the stairs and out the lobby door. It wasn't light yet—they weren't supposed to be outside—but Alan said it was an emergency, and he knew what to do in an emergency. Simon watched them as long as he could from the lobby, ducking back behind the blinds if he thought he saw movement in the street. Then he went back upstairs and waited until dawn for his brother to come back. He waited until he couldn't keep his eyes open any more.

Julie motioned for the root beer bottle again. Simon handed it over and watched her pour the rest of the water over her chin and neck. He rubbed his own cheeks, feeling the stubble scratch his fingertips. "I can't do it," he said.

"You have to."

He looked away, staring at his reflection in the TV screen. TV-Simon looked worried and that made Simon worry too. "You have to take me."

"No, Simon," Julie said. "I'm not going."

A sour taste started to fill the back of his mouth. TV-Simon started to chew on his bottom lip. "I'm not supposed to go alone."

"Yes, you are. This one time. Remember my cousin in St Louis? He's expecting you." Julie's voice began trailing off, but Simon could still hear her say: "It's far away from the ocean."

"The ocean's bad."

"Yes, Simon."

"Alan knows how to drive," Simon said. "He drives the fire truck. He can drive both of us."

"We'll find an automatic car…you know what that means? No shifting. Just brake and steer."

"No!" His heart dropped into his stomach, like he was riding a roller coaster and the car suddenly plunged down a long hill. Those roller coaster cars went fast and spun you around, but they stayed on the track. They stayed on the track because someone was driving them. Someone *else* was driving them.

"You take me!" Simon's heart started pounding. The room began to spin around him—Julie on the couch, then the TV, the doorway to the kitchen, the door to the hallway, back to Julie on the couch. He slapped himself on the side of the head the way Momma used to slap the TV to make *Family Feud* stop jumping on the screen. She could make it work like that—Momma had the touch.

The whole apartment was starting to blur and turn fuzzy, so he hit himself again, harder. From somewhere close by he heard Julie cry out—

"Simon, don't do that!"

He didn't want to, but the squeezing feeling in his chest kept winding the room like a top. "Simple Simon can't do it. Simple Simon can't." He had to say it first—before anyone else—because the words didn't hurt as much that way. "Simple Simon can't!" He hit himself again.

"Simon!" Julie was in front of him now, grabbing at him. Her hands were rough, like sandpaper, around his wrists. They didn't have much strength in them, but this close, her fishie-smell cut a little space through which Simon could see.

"Look at me, Simon, look at me…" Parts of her face around her eyes and across her cheeks were starting to peel like an old sunburn. Instead of pink, the skin underneath was pale—almost gray—but somewhere inside the black-glass marbles staring at him, her eyes were still hers.

The side of his head was throbbing, but the whirlwind had begun to settle down. He wiped his nose with his shirt sleeve. "I'm scared," he said.

"I know. And that's okay. It's okay to be scared."

He closed his eyes and for the length of a heartbeat, he was driving through open country. No buildings crowding over the street, but green land running to the horizon on all sides. Yellow sun. Blue sky. White clouds, and the perfume of blossoms in the air. In the seat next to him—

Simon opened his eyes. "I don't want to be by myself."

"You're not by yourself." Julie helped him to his feet and pulled him close. His legs trembled as if they were cold, knocking against each other and against her legs. But Julie just held on. She hugged him longer than anybody ever—except Momma.

"I love you," he whispered.

Julie nodded. They held each other for a long time.

He made macaroni and cheese for supper, but not real macaroni and cheese because there wasn't any milk to make the cheese sauce with. Julie said to use butter instead, which wasn't right but it turned out okay anyway. Simon ate all of his and most of her bowl after she said she didn't want any more.

By the time the table was cleared, the rain had started to fall. It rapped angrily against the windows when the wind gusted, as if trying to break in. Julie went back to the couch and Simon took his seat in his green chair, wishing that something—anything—would come on the TV. The only thing to look at was TV-Simon, who was looking back and waiting for *him* to do something. But Simon just sat there, listening to the rain and Julie's coughing and slurping for breath. Momma would poke Alan if he snored on the couch, but he thought he shouldn't bother Julie right now because she wasn't feeling good.

A shout from outside made him jump. Simon got up to sneak a peek through the curtains. Noises used to come from the street every night—car tires screaming, people screaming. Sharp, high sounds like the sirens on his brother's fire truck. That was when the TV still worked and they could have a couple of lights on in the apartment if the drapes were closed all the way. Now, he peered outside and thought he did see someone running across the parking lot across the street, headed for the waterfront. Simon shook his head. The fishies were always headed that way, especially when it was dark or wet outside, and right now it was both. Alan used to tell him about the bodies on the boardwalks, the wharves, the streets. Wherever they fell, they were always pointed toward the water.

Stop that, Momma would say. *That's not talk for the table.* And so the boys would wait for Momma to go to her room to read before bed. Alan would turn up the TV, then sneak back to the kitchen to tell Simon everything. About their flaky gray skin that scratched you and made you bleed if you rubbed them the wrong way. Their noses were flat, and their eyes small and black, like the flounder you could catch right off Brewster's Pier. And, just like the flounder, they needed to breathe in the ocean. Alan said the dead ones couldn't get to the water in time. *They drowned in the air!* he said.

Stupid fishies! Simon laughed.

Every morning the bodies kept showing up near the water, especially after a rain. More and more people started wearing hoods and long capes, even when it was sunny. Alan started telling him to come straight home from the Center, and don't even stop at the Citgo station for a Milky Way, and if anyone starts following you, run away fast. *Don't talk to them*, Alan said. *They're turning fishie.*

Momma stopped coming out of her room about the same time that channel 45 went off the air. No more *Family Feud*. Alan said she was sick and needed lots of rest and quiet. She ate all her meals in her room and drank lots of juice and water all day long.

Don't look at her, Alan said once, helping her walk to the bathroom. Simon turned away, but he still could smell her. An oily scent that coated the inside of his nose.

He sighed heavily, shuffling back to his chair from the window. *I wish*, he wanted to say plopping on the cushion, but then thought that wishes were only for birthdays and blowing out candles. For his last birthday, he'd wished for a day at the beach. Momma and Alan swam way far out, bobbing as they waved to him. Simon bathed more in the sun and the clean salt air than the water, and by the end of the day, his arms and legs had turned a warm pink. They stayed until the sun began to paint the sky in streaks of red and orange over the city. On the way back to the car, they turned around for one last look at the ocean. Momma and Alan noticed it first—a muddy stain far away along the horizon.

Smoke from a freighter, Momma said.

Storm front, Alan said.

Stretched across the back seat, feeling the hum of the car on the highway vibrate through his whole body, Simon felt like he was still floating on the waves. Momma and Alan talked softly between the chatter of the Red Sox game on the radio. The slumber he had slipped into then—like the one he was slipping into now—offered a promise of peace. No dreams, no strange sounds in the night. And so Simon didn't fight the pull, but allowed sleep to draw him into its depths and hold him there as long as it wanted.

Sunlight had found a gap through the curtains and poured across Simon's face. In the morning stillness, all he could hear was his own breath whistling through his nose. He rolled his head away from the sun, keeping his eyes closed as if he was still sleeping. In reality, he listened for water running in the bathroom sink, or the toaster popping up toast, or the clink of a spoon in a cereal bowl. Momma used to tease him for being a sleepyhead. Actually, he was always the first one awake but he liked hearing Momma and Alan talk in soft voices, walking lightly from their bedrooms to the bathroom to the kitchen until one of them came to get him.

He waited for them even now—like waiting to hear Santa Claus leaving presents under their ceramic, table-top tree. But he had never once caught Santa in the act, and he didn't hear anyone now in the kitchen, or the bathroom, or anywhere in the apartment.

Simon rubbed his face and rolled himself out of the chair onto his feet. Julie was awake already, too. She was lying on the couch, staring up at the ceiling. She wasn't rasping any more, or making that wet gulping sound. She wasn't…

He bent over her, waving his hand in front of her eyes. They had turned dull and smoky in the night and the lids had pulled all the way back into her head. Her lips were parted as if to whistle, but no sound was coming out. The skin flaps on her neck weren't moving.

Simon bit the inside of his cheek. He lifted Julie by her arms and pulled her into a sitting position where her head could slump against his shoulder. She felt cold and no matter how he rubbed her back or her cheeks, she stayed that way. For a moment, the idea raced through his head that this wasn't really Julie at all, but some other fishie instead. Julie was somewhere else—maybe getting them another car, or finding some milk that hadn't gone bad.

He liked that idea, but couldn't make his arms let go. The air in the apartment settled over him the way that sometimes he let warm wax pour off a candle onto his fingers. For a moment, he was stuck. He couldn't move his arms, or lift his head, or even let the breath out of his lungs. His body too heavy.

Slowly, the air began to leak out of him in a long sob, sawing its way in and out of his chest. Simon let Julie slide back down on the couch, and could see now that she was empty. The same way that the city was empty. The silence around him was complete and total. Even his own thoughts were dying inside his head, smothered by the quiet. He realized it now—that they'd all left him for good. Momma and Alan. Julie. All gone without him.

He felt he was sinking into himself, further and further from the morning light filling the apartment. Everything was hushed now. He could almost go back to sleep.

And just before releasing, he heard it. A voice. Inside of him, but not him.

You have to do it, it said.

Take her to the water, it said.

Simon stood, and like someone was leading him by the hand, he walked into his bedroom, took the top blanket off his bed and wrapped Julie tight, just like he'd seen Alan do for Momma. She was easy to carry all the way down the stairs, through the lobby, and out the door—like the really important part of her had already left. Gone to Heaven.

The overnight storm had scrubbed and polished the sky. Gulls and terns pinwheeled through the air, screaming for the pure joy of it as they followed Simon down to the waterfront. He walked until the glut of abandoned cars in the street became too thick. Switching to the sidewalks got him a few blocks closer before that way, too, became blocked. He had to lay Julie on a hood or trunk, then climb over and pick her up again before he could keep going. It was bad to climb on other people's cars, and it was bad to be this close to the water no matter what the day was like. He closed his eyes and could almost imagine the bird-cries sounding like voices. "Stop that!", they yelled and "Get away!". But there was no one to get mad at him except the birds, and they seemed too happy to be yelling. Here and there, whole bunches of them were even gathered between the cars like they were having a party, but they yammered and flew away when Simon came close.

At last he made it through the last parking lot in front of Brewster's Pier. The morning sun was still climbing over the water, making the tips of the waves sparkle. Alan took him fishing here, or sometimes to go on a boat and watch the whales. They usually saw lots of them just beyond the mouth of the harbor, flapping their tails and blowing bubbles in the water. Simon walked past the whale boats to the end of the pier. Now and then, through the fishie smell, he could catch a bit of sharp, clean sea air. Usually he couldn't see the open water because so many boats were in the way, but they were all gone now. He could look all the way through the harbor and out to the ocean. So enormous and yet so empty.

The lapping sound of the waves against the posts of the pier drew Simon's attention. The water that was a twinkling blue off in the distance looked black and green directly below. He couldn't see his reflection exactly—more like a shadow of himself on the water. But Shadow-Simon had powerful eyes that held him with their gaze. Watching. Waiting.

Simon let his arms release their hold. He heard a splash and looked down. Julie floated for a moment or two before the water pulled on her and started to take her under. Feet first, then the legs and chest. He waited until her head disappeared, sinking into a pale green light just below the surface.

He turned back to face the city. It was so still and so silent that Simon held his breath to make sure he wasn't going to disturb anything. The pale grey buildings stood like monuments—no longer serving a purpose except to mark a place where, once upon a time, something used to happen. Silent now.

Julie had said he needed to find a car. Some might have keys still inside. And check for gas in the tank, he remembered. That was important. And the car needed to be automatic. Just brake and steer (*don't crash!*).

All the way to St Louis.

Tightness spread up from his chest, through his throat and into his face.

You have to do it, his Voice said.

All alone? he asked.

The city skyline swallowed the sunlight. Beyond the knot of cars, he could see only dark canyons snaking their way into the distance. How far did the city go until the road was open? It looked like it lasted as far as he could see. Farther.

He turned back to the water. Below the tips of his orange-and-white sneakers, dark shapes zoomed through the water like torpedoes. Simon waved and Shadow-Simon waved back.

He closed his eyes, and could smell cherry blossoms on the air. And the sea salt. The gulls were chattering all around him—one of them shrieked with laughter. Simon laughed too, as if he'd heard the same joke. He laughed, and laughed, and laughed.

Chilling

Nash felt the right front tire skid just a bit on the ice as he pulled up outside the resident-manager's office for Alba Acres. Just as he switched off the ignition, a sudden gust buffeted the squad car—herald of the nor'easter rushing down from New Brunswick, across Maine, and into Massachusetts. A real brute, the radio had warned. The whole town was battening down for it. Nash knew he and his officers were staring down the barrel of a long forty-eight hours: downed power lines, automobile accidents, and sure enough some idiot would pick this one weekend to hike around Quabbin Reservoir no matter what the weather was doing.

And there was a kidnapping to get it all started. *At Alba Acres?* he thought. Somebody's imagination had to be working overtime; he figured he knew whose. Out of the corner of his eye, he watched a sixty-ish man hobble to the top of the concrete steps leading up from the street.

Nash opened his car door and stepped straight into the winter chill. "Are you Mr. Galloway?"

"Yes, yes, of course I am." Galloway instantly turned and started back the way he had come, favoring his right leg.

Nash hustled up the steps. His boots made crunching sounds on the rock-salt strewn across the sidewalk. "Need a hand, sir?"

"I ain't gonna slip. Damn hip acts up when the storms come through, that's all. Broke it almost thirty years ago on the Ticonderoga trail up there on Mount Mackintosh. You know it?"

"Not much of a skier." The two men entered a small quadrangle enclosed by the four main buildings of the housing complex. Nash pointed across the snow-covered common to a unit with its front window smashed. "Is that Mr. Knowles's?"

Galloway nodded, burying himself in the collar of his coat.

"How long has Mr. Knowles lived here at the home?"

"Assisted living!" spat Galloway. He sucked in a hard breath. "We ain't no whiny, suck-tit nursing home. Every apartment has a full kitchen and bath, living room, bedroom. The folks here are senior, not helpless."

"Uh-huh. So they can come and go as they please?"

"Of course!"

"Then Mr. Knowles might just be out somewhere, staying with family."

"No family. Not no more. Besides, what about the blood?"

Nash put out his hand to block Galloway's path. "What blood?"

"Along the window, all over the ground—look at it!"

Nash stepped in front to look where the older man was pointing. Blowing snow had obscured the droplets, but he could definitely make out frozen splashes of crimson dotting the snow amidst shards of glittering debris. His eyes narrowed curiously. The ground outside, rather than the floor inside, was littered with glass—almost invisible against the snow and ice.

"Would you open the door for me, sir?"

Galloway already had his set of master keys in his hand. He tugged off a thick wool mitten to grasp the proper key.

"Has anyone been in here since you noticed the broken window?"

Galloway gave a negative grunt through the mitten clenched in his teeth. Nash pushed the door open and held it. "Okay, we're going to lock this apartment down. Nobody else in here but me. Why don't you wait for me in your apartment. I'll have a few questions when I'm done."

"Number oh-one-hundred. Just down there." Galloway gestured back the way they had come. He pulled the keys out of the lock and slipped his mitten back on.

The front door opened straight into the living room area, divided from the kitchen on the left by a Formica-topped counter. Nash stepped gingerly inside and took a quick visual inventory. The furniture looked cheap, but in good condition. The surfaces of tables and lamps gave off a faint bleached-lemony scent. The most personally expressive exhibits were the shelves and bookcases containing few actual books, but dozens of knickknacks and framed photographs—none of which looked more recent than the Seventies. Toward the back, near the door to the bedroom, was an open davenport. Notebook papers lay wind-scattered around the desk's legs.

A soft crackling sound made Nash look down at his feet. Snow was everywhere, carpeting the living room in what looked like a perfect one inch depth wall-to-wall. There were no clumps, no drifts. It was even under the furniture. He crouched and dipped his glove into it for a taste. *Real snow*, he discovered, not that artificial ski-stuff. And it was loose and granular while the powder outside was well packed—there hadn't been any fresh accumulation for over a week.

And how could windblown snow be laid out so evenly?

Nash stepped along the wall, crossing to the rear of the apartment. A fresh gust of wind tickled him with slivers of cold. It swirled the papers on the floor—most yellowed and brittle to the touch. They were the only items in the room that seemed out of place, so he gathered them carefully in his evidence bags. The pages on the davenport were more recent, but looked to be part of the same work. All of the pages were covered with red editing marks, thick enough nearly to smother the original words.

He clenched and unclenched his fingers, trying to keep up the circulation. The apartment felt like a pocket of Arctic cold. His knuckles popped loudly and he instinctively heard Elaine scolding him. He smiled, even listening to her tirade about the arthritis he was going to give himself. Her voice in his head jogged a reminder to go out to St. Michael's after the storm and leave fresh flowers.

Unbidden, the image of her lying in the plush coffin filled his mind's eye—frostbitten skin the color of chalk.

"How's it going, Chief?"

Nash whirled about. A broad-shouldered bear of a man with a pepper-gray beard filled the door to the apartment. The bill of a battered Chevrolet ball cap shadowed his eyes, his hands were shoved deep into the outer pockets of his red flannel hunting jacket.

"Chief Lavoie." Nash threw a mask over his expression.

Lavoie smiled sadly. "Storm coming."

"Yeah, a whopper. I've got Marlowe and Corey making sure the town gets ready, but you know those two."

"And you?"

"Well, I was the only one left when the call came in on Mr. Knowles about an hour ago —"

"I know."

An odd light in Lavoie's eyes tickled Nash's curiosity, but he shoved the feeling to the back-burner of his mind as he continued. "Doesn't look like any struggle. And check this out." He crossed back to the window, retracing his footsteps along the outside of the living room. "All the glass is outside. The pieces are too fine for it to have been a rock or something, it looks more like the window just shattered. I can't figure…" His eyes ran along the frame. "You live here now, don't you, Chief?"

"Right up there." Lavoie pointed to the apartment directly overhead.

"Really? Then, did you hear the window go last night?"

"Just the wind." Nash watched his predecessor's eyes pass unblinking over the apartment. "Biggest since '75, they say."

"Yeah." Nash folded Knowles' notebook papers and tucked them into an outer pocket. "There's a little blood outside with the glass, but it might not be Knowles's." He stole another glimpse at Lavoie's eyes—finding a mix of sadness and fear. "Maybe he just got, you know, a little befuddled and walked out his own front door. Then, later in the evening, somebody broke the glass. Some kids or something."

"He's out tonight," Lavoie whispered.

"Excuse me?"

The old chief blinked. "You should find him before he's out all night. Hopefully he just went off with family."

"Mr. Galloway said Knowles didn't have family any more. I'm going to put the word out to people. If he's on foot," Nash headed for the door, "then somebody should spot him in the area. Maybe he's headed someplace familiar like downtown, or the park. I'll be all over town today, so…"

Nash let his sentence trail off as he headed for the way out. Lavoie still blocked the doorway. Nash felt those strange, unwavering eyes stare right through him. Lavoie didn't even seem to notice him there; he just gazed at the scene with the bluish reflection of the snow glowing in his pupils. He finally turned away with a heavy, thoughtful exhale of steam.

"Hey, Ed."

Lavoie stopped.

"You sure you didn't hear anything last night?"

The older man looked up at the cloud-thickening sky. "Storm coming," he answered before walking away.

At six o'clock Campbell Street, the main drag through Chattan Falls, fell under the ghostly glow of streetlights bouncing their beams off the descending snowflakes. The cloud cover had effectively blocked out the sun since four; the storm was parked overhead, packing in on itself to create a heavy, gray-and-black ceiling. The blustering wind which had hurried it to town had vanished, leaving an unnatural stillness. The sky waited, for hours it seemed, all the while doubling and redoubling its strength. It was almost a relief when the snowfall finally began.

At least, Nash observed, fear of the storm was keeping foolishness to a minimum. All morning, the state rangers had chased people off the cross-country trails at Mackintosh Hollow, closing the park gates by two. The radio and local cable channel ran lengthy lists of closings and cancellations, and most businesses showed only dark windows and pulled shades. That was good from a public safety standpoint, but bad for a rumbling stomach. If just one restaurant was open it would save him from having to microwave a burrito from the station's vending machines.

The squad car crept past D'Ampezzo's. The orange "Open" sign was lit, but through the plate glass Nash saw chairs stacked on tables and most of the lights out. A burrito was actually starting to sound tasty when he caught a glimpse of Al D'Ampezzo himself sitting in a booth by the window down at the far end. He was sitting in a booth by the window down at the far end, helping himself to a plate of his own cooking. Nash quickly parked and hopped out of the car.

"Eating the profits?" He stamped the loose snow off his boots.

"Hey!" Al waved. "I was just wondering who was crazy enough to be out driving in this."

Nash picked up a red plastic tray and a set of silverware wrapped in a napkin from the counter. "What do you have that's still hot?"

"Whatever you want. The grill is off, but I'll put it in the thingy in back."

"Thingy?"

"You know," Al put a finger across his lips. "A microwave. Don't tell nobody, okay?"

"My lips are sealed. How about a gyro platter, then. With rice."

Al shuffled back into the kitchen while Nash set his tray on the nearest table. Outside, his squad car was already under a thin covering of snow. It wasn't necessarily falling hard or thick, but it sure was collecting quickly. *And*, Nash reminded himself, *Will Knowles was still out there*: officially missing for about eight hours now. The APB had turned up nothing, he hadn't wandered into any familiar haunts and the hospitals didn't have him. It was starting to look like he really had been taken; or, Nash continued reasoning, like he hadn't simply wandered away but gone someplace specific. That made some sense.

But there was still the matter of the blood and the glass. And the snow. Nash thought he could just keep circling the town until the blizzard buried everything, or try narrowing the search a little. He scooted his chair in to his table and pulled out the notebook papers he'd taken from the apartment. The librarians at the town branch told him that, once, Knowles had been quite the local celebrity: teaching literature classes at Mount Holyoke and publishing his work in all the right magazines. The second coming of Robert Frost, people said. Then it all started to unravel sometime in the late sixties. He stopped writing—stopped getting published anyway—and was dismissed from the college. His wife and children left him; he was perpetually behind in his alimony and child support. He just faded from life, like a walking ghost.

Under the scribbling and editing marks, Nash had found a handful of dates—the oldest being March 15th, 1965. It wasn't exactly his kind of writing, but near as he could tell it was about a couple that get separated. It seemed like the girl left the guy, but it might have been the other way around. In any case, it read more like junior high school crooning than the work of a critically-acclaimed poet. But maybe he was missing the point—*entirely possible*, he conceded with a grunt. He should've thought to ask the librarians about it. Or maybe Chief Lavoie.

But that was part of the puzzle. The older man saw the same bizarre spectacle at the apartment, but like it was something he had *expected* to see. And those cold eyes. Nash had never seen a stare quite like that before. The closest thing it reminded him of were the eyes of a survivor looking back at the accident they'd just walked away from.

Those would've been Elaine's eyes. He could envision her shivering on the roadside, maybe watching the sun setting behind the crumpled Taurus with no other traffic in sight—the other car having peeled out and vanished. What did she do to try to keep herself awake? How long did she last before the weight of her eyelids became just too heavy?

He shook the nightmare image out of his head. His watch read six-fifteen. He'd been planning to grab dinner and then sack out at his office for a couple of hours. But sleep didn't seem all that possible the way his head was churning. He fished his cell phone out of his pocket as Al emerged with a plate full to the edges with spiced strips of lamb, slices of pita bread and a mountain of white rice.

"Who you callin'? You need a date to eat dinner?"

"Business, Al." Nash pulled up Lavoie's number. "Go back to your smoke before I tell everyone about your 'thingy.'"

Al laughed and ambled back to his smoldering stogie. Nash listened to the third ring echo in his ear. *He has to be home. Has to be unless he's out in…*

Someone at the other end finally picked up. "Hello?"

"Hello, Chief, it's Kevin. Listen, I'm sorry to bother you but I've got a couple of quick questions."

"You haven't found Will?"

"No, and I'm starting to get worried with the storm starting up and all."

"What do you mean?"

Nash frowned. "I mean the snow. Look out your window."

"I can see out my window just fine and it's not snowing here. Where are you?"

"Downtown. D'Ampezzo's, you know." Nash shot a glance outside. The snow was falling twice as thickly as he'd ever seen it. Alba Acres was only a couple of miles away to the northeast—right in the storm's path. He remembered the snow in the apartment and icy fingers ran up his back. "It started here almost half an hour ago."

"And no one's found Will yet?" Lavoie demanded. "You're sure of that?"

"Yes, I'm sure." Nash turned away from the open room and lowered his voice. "Ed, what are you trying —?"

"There were papers on Will's desk. Did you take them?"

"Now, how did you —"

"Did you take them!"

Nash considered lying. "You mean the poem? Yes."

"Have you read it?"

Nash's thoughts suddenly split, one side listening to the conversation and the other racing on ahead to try to pencil in the connections. "Yeah, but it didn't make much sense to me. Some of the papers date back more than forty years…"

"Yes, yes," Lavoie muttered.

"The poem. What's it about? Did he —" Nash stopped suddenly. Through the curtain of night and snow, he spied a hunched, coatless figure shuffling down the center of the street. "Jesus. Hang on a second, I think I see him."

"Kevin, don't go out there! Stay inside, for God's sake."

"Chief, what're you —" The lights inside D'Ampezzo's and out in the street suddenly cut out along with the phone. Nash's heart thudded nervously in his chest. The shape in the street had disappeared. A tense quiet settled in. He took a moment, staring into the dark street, to gather himself again.

"Al, you stay put." Nash zipped his jacket and flipped up the collar against the wind as he hurried out the door. Between the snow and the blackout, he could barely see anything further than a foot in front of him. He trudged carefully out into the street, feeling eerily lost without the visual landmarks around him. The buildings had essentially vanished, leaving him alone in the cold and the dark and the thick, swirling snow.

Suddenly, a glow appeared about a hundred yards ahead of him. Nash stared incredulously. It had the same stark white glare of headlights, but it flickered like flame. It was stationary, so definitely not a car, but not coming from any building either. He walked toward it slowly, picking his feet up and out of the drifts, one at a time.

A man-sized shadow suddenly appeared. The glow turned a frosty turquoise as it broke around the silhouette standing like the wick in the heart of a brilliant candle. The light touched Nash's face, warm as sunlight. He shielded his eyes with his hand. The shadow-man was blocking his view of the light source, and yet it didn't seem to matter. A sensation of warmth and welcome filled his veins. The closer he got, the more detail he could make out of the now-kneeling man's features. Nash took a reflexive inventory of the subject: cream-colored turtleneck under a knit cherry-red cardigan, brown dungarees and old L.L.Bean rubber boots. He guessed the man would stand about 5'8", 200 lbs with his pot belly, and was easily between sixty-five and seventy years old. Will Knowles, for certain.

Then, Nash noticed a second person in the heart of the light: a nude woman, also kneeling, and facing the old man with her arms spread open as if to take him into an embrace. Ice-blue hair, as long as she was tall, wafted softly behind her in a phantom wind. Her sheer beauty speared Nash through the chest. She was the light, radiating like a sun amidst the storm-tossed night. Even the snowfall around her sparkled with a diamond brilliance that stopped Nash dead in his tracks, unable to move any closer to the awesome vision. It was Elaine. He knew because his heart was taking the same extra excited beats it had all the times he'd fallen in love with her. She had the same merry twinkle in her eyes, the faint rosiness beneath porcelain cheeks. If he could just hear her speak—listen to her laugh—he could be sure…

A blaring horn slammed into his ears. He turned to catch a blinding eyeful of a pickup's headlights rushing madly toward him. Nash's legs turned to stone. He could only watch the truck bear down on him, then suddenly swerve away. His mind at last reconnected to his body—he threw himself back into the snow just as the truck's rear end swung around. He felt the wind of its passing through the spot where he'd just been standing.

Nash quickly rolled over and up in to a crouch to watch the fishtailing truck go by. The blood drained right out of his face. The momentum was carrying the pickup straight towards Knowles and the woman. Nash put his hand on his 9mm. *To do what?* a tiny rational voice asked. *Shoot the tires?*

Shoot the driver?

The truck spun around almost a full ninety degrees, giving Nash a clear view of Lavoie's panicked eyes. Time stopped. He could act in this preserved instant. The weapon was drawn, but his arms felt like lead. His body couldn't seem to understand the instructions coming from the brain. *Blue can't shoot blue*, said his fingers, his hands, his arms. But a louder voice, one that wasn't entirely his own, shouted down the protests. *Protect*, it said.

Nash brought the weapon up. He didn't recognize anymore the screaming man behind the windshield. *Bring him down.* It was no different than sighting on a mad dog in a schoolyard. *Protect. Protect…*

But by then the instant was gone, rejoining the flow of time. Nash could suddenly see in his mind's eye the moment of impact when the two-tons of steel slam into the beautiful woman, splintering her bones and turning them into a hundred tiny blades with which to slice her heart, her lungs, her guts. She would shower the snow with her blood.

Nash roared. He fired blindly, hitting nothing. At the last moment, he saw Lavoie in the truck cab throw his arms over his face, helpless to do anything but hurtle backwards into his fate.

The pickup was engulfed by the glow. Pure white light erupted like lightning. The frosty blast lifted Nash into the air, the panic of sudden flight filling his chest. He fell blindly backward until he felt his back crash through a plate glass window. His head bounced off the floor, sending sparks of pain knifing through his temples.

He picked himself up, fighting off the blurred, swirling vision. Mannequin torsos and aluminum display trees lay toppled and broken at his feet. Slivers of glass had sliced his parka and left tiny cuts across the exposed skin on his chin and cheeks—not much worse than shaving nicks. He bent for his piece, feeling a sharp twinge in his lower back.

Her. Nash vaulted back into the street over the sharp complaints of his joints and muscles. Darkness had reclaimed the scene, and the snow was flying just as furiously as before. He stumbled blindly forward. Eventually his eyes traced the outline of Lavoie's Chevy—turned on its side and smashed into the brick side of a building down the block, wheels spinning ever more slowly.

His feet stubbed against something in the snow. Nash knelt gingerly to feel for the buried object, trying not to think that it was happening *again*; that it was *her* lying in the road. The silence was so perfect, he heard every flake land on his nylon jacket. The serrated pain in his heart cut him in two. He didn't really want to see, didn't want it to be true…

He uncovered a sweater sleeve. The sight of it brought the thinnest of smiles to his lips. He tugged and pulled it up; underneath was bare pavement, as if the body had been there since the snow had started falling. He brushed off the face. Knowles' frozen expression was heavenly, beaming with a sense of unimaginable peace. Nash set the old man back in the snow and kept looking for Elaine. Her face was already blurred in his memory, just an anonymous shape at their first date, their wedding, the last dinner they'd shared. There had to be something still here, buried in the snow. She couldn't be so utterly *gone*.

Nash stared into the dead man's open eyes, jealousy enveloping his heart. Knowles had seen her—her face was nearly still there in the reflection in his eyes. A chill hooked itself in Nash. The world was darker than night, colder than winter. He fell onto all fours. He stayed down there in the snow for what seemed like hours. When he could rise again, he noticed the storm had stopped. The clouds overhead were in tumult—shadowy masses tumbling over one another like a fleeing mob. A sliver of moonlight burned through. The storm was leaving as quickly as it had come. It was a new knife-thrust through his heart. He felt cut out of the world.

A groaning from nearby stirred Nash with a new, and blacker, desire. His eyes narrowed into stone-cold slits. He stood upright, adjusting the grip of his pistol in his hand. Each step toward the crashed pickup was an effort; the drifts in the street were four feet deep in some places and his body rebelled stiffly against every movement. But a dark fire in his belly heated his blood, making it bubble in his veins. His conscious thoughts stepped aside. He watched himself, as if in a dream, stride the last few feet to the truck and clamber to where he could perch on the driver's side door.

He aimed his automatic through the broken window, eyes straining to find his target.

Lavoie lay crumpled at the bottom of the cab, back against the passenger door. Nash could barely see him amidst the blackness.

"You saw her, dinn't ya?" The older man coughed.

"You bastard." Nash's words dropped icicles.

"Swear to God, I didn't want you to go through —"

"And you left her to die."

"WAIT!"

Nash's finger froze on the trigger.

"I can tell you saw her. I can tell. Will used to get crazy like that from time to time." Lavoie cleared his throat. His voice bubbled. "He and I were old friends, played football together. Then the storm came. I was out on patrol and his brand-new Plymouth had gone off the road out on Old Sheridan Boulevard. I was bringing him back to the station so he could call his family. That's when the storm hit us. Biggest since '38, they said. It was all I could do to stay on the road."

Nash kept his aim on Lavoie's chest.

"Then Will says to me, 'Isn't that Jay Hogan?' Hogan was a miserable old recluse. He owned almost all the property around Prescott Pond and wouldn't let nobody else build there. He was walking down the street with no coat on, eyes fixed straight ahead. Didn't look like he heard us yelling at him or hitting the horn. Will hopped out of the cruiser while I turned around. I couldn't see more than a few feet ahead of me, and I lost sight of the both of them. I turned on my lights, hoping they'd find me. I was just creeping along, hoping I didn't run them down in the street.

"Then I saw the glowing. I had no idea what it was, but I headed straight for it. It was further than I thought, in that storm it felt like it took hours to get close. Just as I did, it winked out and I couldn't see shit again."

Nash kept staring at his target, tracing his shadow amidst the night. The rational voice in his head was bleeding out through his gaze.

"Then I see Will, carrying Hogan dead and stiff as a board. And Will was crying. I mean, bawling like a baby. He kept talking about 'her' and 'she' was gone. He was out of his head, and it scared me. It scared me like nothing else in my life. And he never got better, d'you hear me? He got fired from his teaching job in '77. His wife and kids left him in '79. And his whole life turned into that goddamned poem. For 'her', he said. He showed it to me couple times, usually when he was drunk. Kept saying 'she' was coming back. Last week I knew he was right. Worst storm in forty years, they said. And I knew."

"You never saw her." Nash's voice blew a fresh chill into Lavoie's bones.

"I never did."

"You never loved her."

"No, I did not."

"You never lost her." Nash's finger tightened on the trigger.

"No."

"It feels like this."

The first booming report of the gun surprised him. It awakened Nash for a moment, but by that time there had been a second shot, and a third. Each pull on the trigger came easier than the last. He watched Lavoie's body shudder with each impact, dancing like a coffee can out in the woods—*pop, pop, pop!* He didn't register it at first when the magazine was empty. He kept pulling the trigger over and over until his knuckle was sore. Then he stopped, and turned away without looking down into the cab.

He sat on the truck's door, legs dangling over the side, and reloaded. The sky above was now cloudless, and the moon wore a milky haze around its snow-white brilliance. It shone so bright, without the streetlights and store lights to wash it out. *Storm coming*, he repeated like a mantra. He pointed the gun toward a sudden sound. Someone was trudging through the snow toward him, calling his name. *Protect.* He could do that. Protect her from the snow and the ice and the driver who didn't stop. A sudden chill would be her sign, and she would lay a path for his feet as clean as a carpet of perfect snow. He would do what she needed done, and be what she needed him to be.

A cold tear scalded his cheek.

Storm coming.

Miss Cavern Queen

"**T**here it is!"

Hadley looked up from her iPhone in time to glimpse the blue billboard her mother was pointing at just before they zipped past it.

"Welcome to Kentucky," she repeated and tried to copy her mother's smile. The muscles in her lower back had worked themselves into yet another bind within the last fifty miles, and no matter whether she slouched in the car seat or sat straight as a flagpole, the knot stayed right where it was. It had actually begun tying itself overnight in the hotel back in Harrisburg. Elegant room, all the amenities and services one could want, but with mattresses like stone slabs. After having awoken out of discomfort for the fourth time, Hadley wondered if she'd have been better off sleeping on the floor.

"Well," her mother said, "I wonder if we'll have to show our passports."

Hadley rolled her eyes. While her mother may be thinking that driving from New England to Kentucky constituted a voyage to a foreign country, the landscape outside their Escalade windows all seemed the same to her. Every time she dozed off, her first wish upon awakening was to see something truly different. But, there was the same Target store to greet her, and the same Burger King, and Best Buy, and so on. Even now, near journey's end, it was hard to accept that she and her mom had actually travelled anywhere at all. The grass didn't even look any different—wasn't the grass in Kentucky supposed to be blue?

Don't know why we bothered, she thought, and sighed louder than she'd intended.

"What?" Ivy asked, although Hadley suddenly had a gut feeling that her mind had just been read. A stranger wouldn't have noticed any change, but Hadley could see her mother's jaw lock closed and her cheeks flush ever so slightly.

"Nothing."

Ivy's mouth twitched a couple of times before she was able to immobilize the tic in a smile and hold it on her lips. "You know, I can't remember my mother ever taking me on a trip like this. Just two girls and the open road." She clucked her tongue and glared at the interstate, as if the pavement had done something wrong. "Of course, it wasn't really possible. Your grandmother worked as a dispatcher for a bus company, you know."

"I remember," Hadley said politely.

"A good job, one of the best a woman in your grandmother's position could get. And any time she didn't want to work, there was a line of people waiting for her job. I would have loved to have gone on a vacation with her. I would have loved for us both to take a week and have an adventure. But then, we would've come home to go stand in the welfare line. And, poof!" Ivy slapped the steering wheel. "There would've gone my chance at Miss Massachusetts, and poof! there would've gone the scholarship, and where do you think we would be? Not in this nice car. Not with your iPhone and your dresses and your—"

"I'm sorry," Hadley said, and a part of her even meant it. But honestly, it was more about cutting to the end of her mother's lecture than anything else. She'd learned to do that by watching her father, and the way he could salvage a strategic retreat from open ground when Mother started hurling thunderbolts of moral superiority.

The tactic didn't always work, but this time Ivy's mouth did relax its tension, and she let out a steady breath—not a sigh, but rather a controlled release of pressure. "I understand you've got nerves, but you need to just get rid of them."

"Yes, Mother."

"Judges are like dogs, they smell fear. They identify the weak and weed them out right away. You have to be a winner from the moment you walk in." Ivy shot Hadley a sideways glance. "You're a winner."

Hadley nodded, but that wasn't the response her mother was looking for. "Say it, Hadley."

"I'm a winner."

"Say it and mean it this time."

"I'm a winner!"

"What will you win?"

"Miss Cavern Queen!"

"Yes you will!" Now Ivy smiled one of her own pageant-winning smiles: the one that made her Miss Teen Massachusetts and Miss Massachusetts once upon a time, now turned into the primary weapon in the marketing arsenal of Bay Colony Home Furnishings. Six stores from Gloucester to Foxboro (plus one across the border in Providence) handed down through Hadley's father's side of the family. As a business, it mostly broke even—thanks to Ivy Devon's grace and charm in almost twenty years of television commercials. But the backbone of the "empire" (as it were) was interior design for high-end clients, and Hadley knew that branch of the company was all about her mother. She'd married into the name and prestige of a classic New England family, but wore the mantle of it ten times better than her husband ever did.

"It's the beginning for you, dear," Ivy continued. "The next level."

Hadley bit her lip. "I just don't know if it'll mean anything back home."

"Of course it won't mean anything back home! Don't bite your lip," Ivy said. "I did a Google search and found the most remote, bush-league, off-the-beaten track pageant in the country. No website, hardly any press coverage at all. They don't even hold it every year."

"Then what's the point?"

"It's for you." Ivy reached over and put her hand on her daughter's shoulder. "To rack up an easy title, feed your inner winner. Winning and losing are both about momentum. Once you start winning, it gets easier to keep winning."

Hadley called up one of her own practiced smiles—bright yet modest, which was one of the trickiest combinations to pull off but also the most important. Ivy smiled back, and through the sides of her sunglasses, she winked. "That's my girl."

The SUV suddenly lurched to the right. "And here we are!" Ivy declared. Hadley breathed a quick sigh of relief that the one lane between their Escalade and the interstate exit towards Holden Hill had been empty. At the end of the exit ramp, another sign pointed them east and promised the town of their destination was only five more miles. While her mother started humming in excitement (a tune Hadley didn't recognize whatsoever), she concentrated on keeping her smile screwed in place. The pit in her belly was spreading, growing deeper and deeper until she thought she might just fall into herself. And wouldn't that please Mother to no end if her prize daughter dissolved into jelly the moment she opened the car door. Guilt mixed with the anxiety already swimming in her heart and made the twisting road they were on feel like one of those Six Flags super roller coasters—spinning and twirling in three different directions at once before suddenly hurtling off in some entirely new direction.

Her smile was her only anchor, the mask providing the only comfort. And so she kept on smiling (*like a fucking idiot*, she thought) as the road turned down a steep decline. The town of Holden Hill actually lay in a valley. One main street ran through the middle of a mile-long downtown. If there had actually been a hill under the town once, it must have collapsed into a pocket amongst its sisters. Hadley could feel the shadows of the land overcoming the sunlight as they descended. She looked at the trees—they became progressively shorter and thinner the deeper into the hollow they went.

"There." Ivy pointed to the right just before the road dropped one last time, and Hadley caught a glimpse of a large fairground with three long pavilions at the near end by the main entrance. Once they reached the valley bottom, Ivy steered them in that direction, following a path of bright ribbons and crepe paper animals festooning the streetlamps. Every storefront was draped in banners—either traditional red, white, and blue, or maroon and white (which seemed to go with the colors of

the sign they saw standing in front of Cavern Country High School).
The whole town was decked out for a massive celebration…except for
one thing.

"Where is everybody?" Hadley asked.

"At the fair, I suppose. Town like this, it's probably the most excitement they get all year."

Hadley continued to stare at the buildings as they drove by. Every
one had crumbly, cracked façades—peeling paint, worn brick—that had
borne the beatings of many years. The wind and the rain had taken the
edges off everything, rounded every corner like the hills themselves.
A quaint, picturesque town from a distance, but dead as a museum.
The streets were empty, the windows of the stores and houses looked
empty, as if abandoned in the middle of the party. Like one of those
ghost ships she read about in school—no sign of distress or emergency,
just…empty. Left to float (or, in the case of Holden Hill, left to sit) in
the midst of the Kentucky hills. Unnoticed and unnoticing.

The first sign of any life at all appeared when Hadley and Ivy arrived
at the gravel parking lot of the fairgrounds. Ivy found a spot close to
the main pavilions that was more grass than rock, between two heavy
pickups. Hadley opened her door, and without the filtered air-conditioning of the Escalade, nearly doubled over from the swampy air and
the smell. It wasn't the usual dung and musk smell of a county fair. This
was earthier…more musty…like a long-forgotten chamber where the
trapped air inside had been baked, then frozen, over and over for more
than a hundred summers and winters, flavored by something slowly
rotting.

She looked over to her mother, who also had a well-rehearsed smile
set in place. They shared a look that was as clear as words before walking in step to the main gate. No one was on duty in the little ticket shed,
so they headed for the nearest pavilion where there seemed to be some
indication of activity. The inside had been sectioned off, the front third
or so ringed with folding tables and chairs. Through a gap in some
curtains, Hadley could see (and smell) stalls for livestock. She breathed
shallowly, but actually discovered the odor was not as strong inside the

building as she'd expected. Just the opposite, in fact, as if being indoors was keeping something out.

She turned around and jumped. "Oh!"

Just inside the door, a girl was sitting in a wheelchair. At first glance, Hadley thought it was an elderly woman, but without the wrinkles. She was, however, a girl—maybe a few years older than Hadley herself—although her skin was beyond pale. It looked dry and brittle, like the bark of a paper birch. Her hair, which once might have been a vibrant strawberry, was now a dull rust color and plastered itself to her cheeks and neck from sweat. The girl looked thin as a stick, except for her belly, which sat like a beach ball between her cupped hands.

"Mom?" Hadley said weakly, and Ivy stepped in to crouch at the side of the wheelchair. The girl's eyes didn't seem to acknowledge either one of them—she just stared ahead at nothing in particular.

"Sweetheart," Ivy said gently, "are you here with somebody?"

Hadley didn't think they were going to get a response, but before her opinion could be verified, a lanky gentleman came through the part in the curtains. A faded blue ribbon dangled from one hand, and he stopped short upon seeing two strangers.

"Anna?" he said to the girl in the wheelchair.

Ivy stood and smoothed the front of her skirt. "Hello. I take it the young lady is with you?"

"Yes, ma'am," the man said. "Something I can help you with?"

"The Cavern Queen pageant." Ivy made a subtle motion with her hand to bring Hadley to her side.

"Pageant?" the man repeated.

"Yes. Your pageant here at the fair." Ivy bumped the brightness of her smile up another level until Hadley could see the light reflected in the man's eyes. Suddenly, though, she had a flash of feeling intensely out of place in her slacks and blazer, and Ivy dressed in black Capris with a *Roman Holiday* scarf around her neck, standing on the straw-strewn floor and breathing in the smell of cattle with every breath. And yet, as her mother would remind her, *Beauty is Beauty anywhere She goes* and this is, after all, what they were here for.

"Pardon me," the man said, "I mean no offense, but I don't believe I recognize you. Who's your family?"

"My name is Ivy Devon, from Massachusetts. This is my daughter, Hadley."

"Collins," the man said, reaching out to shake Ivy's hand but getting Hadley's instead. Another one of Mother's life-lessons—*Never miss an opportunity for a good impression.*

"Mr. Collins," Hadley said with a smile.

"Uh…" Collins faltered.

From the look in his eyes, Hadley could sense his mind spinning to cover the ground that had apparently opened up between real-time and his ability to process what was happening. It was a situation Hadley knew her mother practically drooled over in a business negotiation. Ivy likened it to a prizefighter getting his opponent bloody and against the ropes from the first bell and never letting him out.

And yet, Hadley sensed it wasn't because Collins was dumb in any way, but actually had quite a lot running through his head all at once. *How complicated can this be?* she wondered.

"Hello." A second man entered the pavilion from behind Hadley and her mother. His voice was deep, like a lion's purr, and he was built like a rain barrel with arms and a head. What neck he might have had was obscured by a thick beard the color of a winter sky mere minutes before a storm.

He bowed ever so slightly. "My name is Mr. Cahill. May I help you?"

"I'm sure you can," Ivy answered. Hadley took an inner step back out of the line of fire. Some instinct told her, as it must have informed her mother too, that someone in authority had just arrived. "My daughter and I are here for her to compete in your pageant for Miss Cavern Queen."

"I see," Mr. Cahill said.

"They're from outside the county," volunteered Collins.

"And unless you have a specific provision limiting competition to county residents," Ivy said, "then there shouldn't be any problem."

"Provisions tend to get one bound up in…ah…details instead of the big picture. We prefer to think in terms of traditions," said Mr. Cahill.

His eyes met Hadley's directly—rich, blue eyes. Not intense so much as deep.

She concentrated on not flinching. *Confidence*, she told herself. *Poise. Just how a Queen should be.*

"And traditions are living things that can adapt far more easily than rules or regulations," Mr. Cahill continued. "Collins, Anna looks like she's in need of some food. Would you attend to that, please?"

Collins nodded and wheeled Anna out through the front entrance. "There are some who do not...ah...deal well with the unexpected," Mr. Cahill said with a nod to the now absent Mr. Collins. "Perhaps you know people like that yourself, Mrs. Devon."

"As a matter of fact, I do."

Mr. Cahill gestured to a couple of folding chairs, waiting for Ivy and Hadley to seat themselves before settling on one himself. "Please indulge my curiosity," he said, "but how did you hear of us all the way up in Massachusetts?"

"How did you know where we were from?" Hadley blurted in surprise. Ivy glared at her while Mr. Cahill chuckled.

"I noticed your license plate in the parking lot, miss. It rather stands out for its rarity."

"And that's how your pageant caught our eye, too," Ivy said. "It's rather rare in its own right."

"Yes, it is. And you found out about it...how?"

"Internet."

"Of course."

"Although we couldn't find any contact information or registration materials for the pageant," Ivy said. "Just a mention on the fair schedule."

"Like I said, we've run things more on tradition than rules. It never occurred to us that folks from so far outside Holden Hill would be interested." Mr. Cahill leaned back and studied Hadley and her mother for a moment. "But you two climbed into your car and drove all the way here based on a vague Internet reference?"

"When you put it that way," Hadley jumped in, "I suppose it does sound odd. But it was one of those impulse decisions. Like a....a leap of faith."

Mr. Cahill's gaze hopped for a moment to Hadley's mother, then back to her. In that instant, all the right switches inside his head seemed to click. "Indeed. A leap of faith," he repeated. "That's good. That's very, very good to hear."

He reached for a clipboard with a blank piece of lined notebook paper on it. "Let's make this happen, shall we?"

He scribbled a list of basic information needed, then handed the clipboard to Ivy. "What are the competition categories?" she asked.

"None," Mr. Cahill answered. "Women of your experience with pageants will find us...ah...uncomplicated. The judges meet with all the girls starting at 10 am tomorrow and decide from there based on a total...ah...impression."

"Can you be a little more specific?" Ivy pressed. "What are you looking for in a Cavern Queen?"

Mr. Cahill smiled apologetically. "It's so very hard to put into words. It's a decision...made in the moment. Through inspiration, if you will. A 'leap of faith.'" The last sentence he directed straight at Hadley. "Many of our Queens have come from surprising places. It's not something you can achieve, do you understand? You either are...or you're not."

"Well," Ivy said, rising from her seat. Mr. Cahill made it to his feet faster somehow, and was already reaching to accept her hand even as she'd just begun to offer it. "I suppose our next order of business will be to find a place to spend the night."

"You'll probably have more luck with one of the hotels a little further down the interstate. But before you go," Mr. Cahill said, reaching into his jacket pocket, "Miss Hadley will need this."

He held out a white ribbon, the same style as the one Anna had been wearing, but obviously brand new. Hadley accepted it and immediately turned it over to her mother.

"That will let people know you're one of the contestants," Mr. Cahill explained while Ivy pinned the ribbon to Hadley's blazer just above her left breast. "With it, you'll have free entry to the fairgrounds and all the rides. As often as you wish."

"Thank you," Hadley said.

"Yes, thank you," Ivy added with a pat on Hadley's shoulder, "but I think we'll pass on the rides. Until later."

"Yes," Hadley agreed quickly, "but thank you again for the opportunity."

"It's our pleasure to serve." Mr. Cahill shook hands with both women. "Until tomorrow, then. And I look forward to what inspiration you will bring, Miss Hadley."

Hadley and her mother smiled again, then went back outside to their car. "So very hard to put into words." Ivy mimicked once they were well beyond the fairground gates. "A pageant without a mission statement—whoever heard of such a thing?"

"What do we do?" Hadley asked.

Ivy took a few steps away from her daughter, walking out into the middle of the parking area. Her eyes swept the grounds like a general surveying the field of battle. "We are not going to let a little home-field advantage work against us—that is one thing we are not doing." She looked back to the main gate and the ticket booth. "Mr. Cahill said you could get in to the fair for free. I think that's exactly what you should do."

"Shouldn't I be getting ready for tomorrow?"

"And that's what you'll be doing. Walk around, check out the local character. Every pageant is about *something*, and I don't care what that man says, Miss Cavern Queen is about *something* too and you're going to find out what that is." Ivy stepped back towards her daughter to take her head in her hands, lifting Hadley's face so their eyes met. "This isn't playtime, you understand? Work for this, Hadley. Want this. Want it more than the other girls."

"I will, Mother."

"I'll find us a hotel, then call you. Your cell have plenty of charge?"

Hadley took her iPhone out of her bag. "No signal."

"Damn." Ivy flipped open the cover of her own phone. "Must be this valley. All right, it's four o'clock now. I'll meet you here—right here—at seven."

"Yes, Mother."

Ivy climbed in the SUV and started the engine. "Be a winner!" she called as she closed the door.

"I will!"

Hadley watched the Escalade drive away, kicking up a cloud of dirt and gravel in its wake. Only after it had turned the corner was she reminded of the heat of the day, and the moist patches beginning to form under her arms. As she walked toward the fairground gates, she started planning to find a cool, shaded bench somewhere within. Sitting there probably wasn't what her mother had in mind by "absorbing local character" but she couldn't make a good impression walking around and making a sweaty mess out of herself.

Three things, she told herself. She would find three things that stood out as being different from the fairs back home and that would be enough to report back. Ideally, she thought, she would be able to wander unnoticed up and down a couple rows of booths and displays—just one more anonymous visitor to the fair. No one here could possibly know her, or her family, which meant no expectations of how she was supposed to be. She could say "hello" to someone without being seen as ingratiating, or not say anything at all without being thought of as stuck-up. She could even be allowed to not remember someone's name (a cardinal sin in her mother's world).

Mother was the true celebrity. Hadley knew she was only a celebrity-in-waiting. In-waiting for some time now, in fact. Back home, she could feel the eyes upon her, watching as if she would bloom at any instant. But the longer people looked, the more Hadley was sure that the magnificent event they were looking for would never happen. The more that success was desired, the further it got pushed away.

But, as Hadley approached the ticket booth, it became plain that even here there would be no anonymity. The white ribbon pinned to her blazer caught the eye of the attendant there immediately. He did not smile, but nodded slowly as she approached. With one open hand, he waved her through the gate.

Surprisingly, once inside, the fair seemed just as empty as the town had been. Hadley stood at the head of a long road running straight down the middle of the grounds with tightly packed booths and canopies lining the sides. All the vendor spots appeared to be well-stocked with wares—wood-carved toys in one, the next one over offering copper lawn decorations and birdbaths. Two different booths—both selling hand-made soaps and lotions—faced off against each other from opposite sides of the road. From a little further away, the warm breeze was setting off a symphony of wind chimes. But for all the goods available for sale, no one was around to shop and Hadley only briefly caught glimpses of any vendors stationed to make a sale even if there were.

A wave of uneasiness washed through her. Everything about her seemed to scream "Outsider!", from her clothes to her hair, even to where she was standing—because if she really belonged, then she'd know where she was supposed to be. She needed to go someplace—any place, just so she didn't look like a lost child in front of the main gates. Straight ahead, the tops of roller coasters and tilt-a-whirls peeked over the booths and buildings, but they looked just as abandoned as the display booths. The animal buildings were on her left, and she didn't want to run into either Mr. Collins or Mr. Cahill again looking so confused, so Hadley turned right and went in search of a setting where she could blend in for a while, without looking like she was looking for a setting where she could blend in.

After the last row of booths, Hadley came to a large tent pitched over a grassy area and covering long lines of picnic tables. Here she found a drink stand with a kindly-looking elderly woman actually standing by the cash register. Hadley asked for a medium-sized lemonade (*Fresh-Squeezed!* according to the sign), and when she started to bring out her wallet, the woman behind the counter held up her hands and shook her head. Then, with an almost shy smile, she set the lemonade in front of Hadley and turned away.

"Thank you," Hadley said to the old woman's back. She brought her drink halfway down one of the rows of tables and sat. Now, at last, she began to relax. She didn't feel out of place so much—anyone could see she was sitting down to enjoy her lemonade (which really did taste freshly squeezed) and that wasn't strange for someone to be doing at a fair at all. *Not even*, Hadley thought, *a fair where lots of stuff had been set up for no one to come to.* She looked once again back towards the empty booths, and the empty rides, and thought that seven o'clock was a terribly long time away.

"Pardon me."

Hadley turned around. A young girl—her own age—was sitting on the picnic bench across the row, almost as if she'd appeared there. She must've come up from behind, gliding instead of walking, to have taken a seat so close without Hadley's noticing. Indeed, she was so thin and delicate that she might just have floated on the summer breeze and settled on the bench like a stray leaf.

"Pardon me," the girl said again with a soft accent. Not a drawl, but a pleasant smoothing of all the sounds.

"Yes?" Hadley answered.

The girl's eyes turned downward for a moment, as if the courage to continue lay on the ground between her feet. "Why are you wearing boy's clothes?"

The question almost made Hadley laugh in surprise. Quickly, though, she put the question into context—comparing her suit to the sundress her new acquaintance was wearing. A common red color, draped like a curtain down to her knees and not at all a match for the weathered canvas shoulder-bag slung at her side. Overall, though, she was a pretty girl: mouse-brown hair hanging straight to the nape of her neck, lightened throughout by the same natural sun exposure which had tanned the tops of her shoulders and arms.

"Oh, I quite like it," the girl continued. "I saw an outfit like it once on *The Today Show*. But I've never seen someone wearing it, y'know, in real life." She extended her hand. "I'm Karalee."

"Hadley Devon."

Karalee grinned. "You ain't from here?"

Even though the tone of Karalee's voice rose at the end of the sentence, Hadley understood that she wasn't really being asked a question—and even if she were, this little girl would probably have been crushed if the answer was anything but "yes". So she nodded in the affirmative and Karalee's smile got even brighter.

"I knew it," she said with a note of victory in her voice. "I knew it."

Hadley pointed to the ribbon pinned on Karalee's dress. "You're in the pageant, too?"

For a moment, confusion flickered in Karalee's eyes. *What do they call it down here if it's not a "pageant?"* Hadley wondered. "For Cavern Queen," she added.

"Oh yes." That extra reference appeared to right the listing ship in Karalee's thoughts. "You've come for it, too, all the way from…?"

"Massachusetts."

For a moment, based on how wide Karalee's eyes grew, Hadley thought she might've said "Mars" by accident. "Glory be," Karalee said. "It's a powerful dream, ain't it?"

"Yes." Hadley folded her hands in her lap. "Well, it's my mother's dream too."

"Your Momma's?"

"She was a beauty queen. I mean, she was, like, The Beauty Queen. And me…I'm not anything. Not yet. I mean, I'm someone, but I don't know who." Hadley clipped her lips shut. *What are you doing*, she scolded herself in her mother's voice, *blabbing to the competition?*

"But in the dream," Karalee said, "it's like you…glow. And the folks around you, they glow. Not as much as you, but some."

A vision of what Karalee was describing danced in Hadley's mind, reminding her of one of those Disney princess fantasies. A party. A ball. Swirling gowns and soft lights. Music. And a crown on her head so dazzling that it lit her face in a halo.

"Yeah, the glow," she laughed. "Oh, I can't believe I'm saying this to someone I just met."

"No, honey." Karalee reached over to take both of Hadley's hands in hers. "I get it. I woke up today with this knot in my belly like the first time I had to babysit my brother all by myself. We spent the whole night staring at each other—him waitin' on me to do something and I don't know what."

"Yeah," Hadley said.

"Yeah," Karalee said. "I think that's why I thought it was okay to come talk to you. I thought you looked like you was feeling the same as me."

She sat back. "I hope you don't mind—I didn't mean nothin' by saying that."

"No, no." Hadley found herself smiling again. "You're totally right. It's like I don't even know what I'm doing here."

"It's the calling. You have to come."

Hadley blinked. Her first thought was that it was quite a leap to refer to being in a beauty pageant as a "calling", but maybe it wasn't so wrong to think that way after all. She'd always thought she was meant to be a Beauty Queen: Miss Junior Eastern States, Miss Junior Teen, Miss American Coed. She couldn't think of a time when it wasn't her dream, and every time she came up short of the crown it felt like dying just a little. Sooner or later, it would add up and actually kill her—and if feeling that way didn't make it a "calling", then she couldn't imagine what would.

"Yes," she said, looking at Karalee and seeing not so much as a shadow of a doubt in the other girl's eyes. "So we've come. Here we are. Now what?"

"Well, I think tonight's supposed to be about one last night of fun. Y'know—bunch of girls cruisin' for a good time."

"How much fun are we supposed to have?" Hadley asked. "You're practically the only other person I've seen in this whole place."

"Yeah," Karalee nodded. "Don't make a lot of sense to me either. There are other girls around, it's just that we all know each other already from school and stuff. So, everybody goes off and does their own thing."

"But where's everyone else? Rest of the town?"

"I think they have the idea it's all more fun if there's no one else around. That way we can act up if we want to and nobody'll say nothin'." Karalee's eyes looked off in the distance. "Just makes me feel lonely."

They sat in silence for a minute more, with Hadley watching Karalee watch something a thousand yards away. "So," she finally said, "what should we do to get crazy?"

"Crazy?"

"Yeah." Hadley looked around for something to give her an idea. "Talk crazy, dance crazy, eat crazy. Tons of ice cream. And pizza."

"Ice cream on top of pizza!" Karalee shouted.

"Yeah!"

"Kiss a boy!"

"Kiss two boys and watch 'em fight!"

They both broke up laughing—loud, cackling laughter. *Undigni-fied*, Hadley's inner voice said. *Go screw yourself*, Hadley said back. She picked up her lemonade cup and put her lips to the straw. Movement close to her hand caught her attention. Then two long, black-tipped legs stepped from the back of the cup onto her hand, followed by two more, and two more, and two more. A yellow and black spider stood on the back of her hand, nearly half as big as her hand itself. Hadley tried to shriek, but she couldn't even catch enough breath to do that. She leapt to her feet, dropping the drink cup which splashed ice and lemonade across her shoes and ankles. The hand with the spider on it was held out as far from her body as she could manage, and Hadley was caught between wanting to shake the creature off and worrying that she'd get bit if she tried.

Suddenly Karalee was at her side, holding her other hand. "Easy, easy," she whispered calmly. "Don't move."

Hadley did her best to freeze, but her body wouldn't stop shaking. The spider was now walking across her wrist and on to the cuff of her blazer. There, it stopped and Hadley would've sworn by anything that it looked at her with a gaze like sunlight peeking momentarily through passing clouds. A minute ticked by like an hour, and then when it seemed as if the creature was done with its study, it leapt to the picnic table and dropped out of sight through a knot-hole in the middle.

"Oh, Hadley." Karalee's voice was hushed with something like amazement. Hadley, on the other hand, was still feeling the vile thing crawling across her skin, and the same tingling quickly travelled across every square inch of her body.

"Yecch!" she cried, shaking her limbs as if she could fling the sensation away.

"No one would believe us," Karalee said, and her eyes had that far-off look in them again. "Even if we tol' them, no one'd believe it."

"I believe I almost peed myself."

"Oh no, honey," Karalee said. "It's the Good News, the Good News." She lunged forward and wrapped up Hadley in a bear hug. "You wanna get crazy now?"

"Oh yeah."

"Let's get crazy. I can get crazy with you. Sure I can." Karalee stepped back and there was an extra light beaming in her face. *Inspiration*, Hadley remembered Mr. Cahill saying. For whatever reason, it had certainly struck her new friend.

"Come with me?" Karalee asked.

"Sure," Hadley said. "Where?"

Karalee giggled and somehow her joyous smile became a hundred watts brighter. "Ain't afraid of heights, are ya?"

The passenger car crested the top of the Ferris wheel then came to a stop, which made it sway generously back and forth. Hadley tightened her grip around the safety bar across her lap until the car and her stomach both settled down. On the ride up, she'd looked mostly through the steel framework of the giant wheel, but now she was staring out over the expanse of the valley, and was acutely aware of every inch of the two hundred feet between her and the ground. The one time she'd dared to look straight down, she could suddenly imagine what it might be like to fall—hurtling faster, faster, faster!—until she hit the earth and splattered like an old tomato.

"Oooh, it makes my feet tingly," Karalee said.

"It's pretty up here," Hadley observed. She could see the eastern fringes of Holden Hill where the houses gradually spread further and further apart before almost disappearing entirely amidst a patchwork of farms. Along the surrounding hills, trees covered the slopes in staggered rows, some of them growing perpendicular to the hillside, as if they'd started on level ground before suddenly pitching to the side.

"Have you ever done this before?" Karalee asked softly. On the ride to the top, her bubbly excitement had muted into a quiet serenity, and now that the valley had come into view, she curled herself into the far corner so she could alternate glances between Hadley and the great expanse below.

"Once," Hadley answered. "Back home. But I don't like heights."

"Me either. But now, somehow, it doesn't seem like such a big deal." Karalee's gaze wandered to the valley below, but Hadley could see her mind hard at work, like she was trying to solve some complicated geometry problem in her head. "Last time I was up here," she continued, "my granddaddy took me. I was so scared, but he had his arm around me the whole time. He was strong, even when he was older. Used to mine here."

"I see the farms." Hadley said. "Where are the mines?"

"Right under us. The whole valley. Well, before it was a valley."

"Oh!" Hadley laughed. "So the name 'Holden Hill' wasn't just somebody being ironic?"

Karalee stared blankly at her. "Somebody wasn't just making a joke?" Hadley explained.

"Not the way Granddaddy told it," Karalee said. "My folks didn't like him tellin' tales 'cuz they said he was remembering stuff wrong. But he never forgot a thing in his life. You could see it in his eyes."

She paused for a moment, staring at the horizon before continuing. "Granddaddy took me up here the last time they picked a Cavern Queen. He never said so, but I figured out later he wanted to tell me things where no one else could hear. There was some stuff I should hear from him because he'd actually been there. Used to be, he said, there was no valley here, and everybody worked in the mines. Goin' after coal. Him, his brothers, and their daddy. The tunnels went way deep."

"How deep?" Hadley asked.

"They used to say 'as far down in the ground as the sky is high.'" Karalee shook her head. "Took half a day just to get where they needed to dig, and from there they kept following the veins deeper and deeper. Granddaddy said they didn't know. They kept digging, until one day they went too far." Her voice dropped suddenly. "And then God got angry."

The last words hung in the air, and Hadley could see that Karalee was as rigid as a statue in her seat—the playful fear of the tall Ferris wheel now replaced by the real thing.

"God?" Hadley prompted.

Karalee nodded. "The sun didn't shine for six days straight. And the town began to sink. Granddaddy said some folks ran away, but the rest knew somethin' had to be done. Who knew if God was going to stop once he'd swallowed Holden Hill? He might take the whole county, or the whole state, or the whole country."

Hadley's mind spun like a top from trying to stay with what she was hearing. The kind of thing her friend was describing was out of one of those SyFy Channel disaster movies, except that Karalee obviously believed every word of it. "And then what?" she asked. *Maybe*, Hadley thought, *it'll make sense by the time she's all done.*

Karalee took a deep breath. "Granddaddy said that once upon a time, somebody had to do something. Somebody special." And then she stopped talking, and just sat with an expression on her face as if the least movement would attract some unwanted attention. The feeling was contagious—Hadley caught herself feeling the soft hairs on her arms and across the back of her neck start to stand on end. Somehow, somewhere below them, an eye had turned their way, not unlike the way the spider had gazed at her before. She was used to being studied, examined, even consumed, by those watching her. But this gaze didn't stop at her skin. It seemed to get inside her, down into places Hadley wanted to keep utterly private. The world could have her on the outside but her heart and soul were supposed to belong only to her.

She tried to turn her attention away from the gaze and ignore it—see if that would make it go away—and noticed that Karalee was speaking again, this time in a low monologue directed at no one in particular. Hadley reached over to touch her hand. "Karalee?"

Karalee stopped mumbling and turned to face Hadley. "I have something to show you," she said while reaching for her handbag. "I wasn't sure if I should show it to anyone, but you and me…well…"

She had the handbag on her lap now, her hands holding something inside it. "I think it's okay now. I was scared before, and then when the

Little One appeared…I guess I'm still scared. So many people need so much, y'know? But that's why we were called. When you're called, you've been chosen, and then you have to be what they need."

Karalee lifted her hands out of her bag. At first, Hadley thought it was part of some kind of trick—that there was nothing in her new friend's grasp at all. Then, something in her hands caught the sunlight. A glint at first. Then a sparkle, and then a dazzling shower of light appeared. Karalee was lifting a gossamer veil in front of her face—the most delicate and vibrant beauty Hadley had ever seen. The sinking sunlight didn't just shine on the veil, it set it to dancing. Karalee looked as if she were standing behind a crystal waterfall.

"I found this when I went out for my chores this morning," Karalee said, "lying on the grass, surrounded by the dew." She smiled shyly while all Hadley could do was stare. Right before her eyes, Karalee had transformed into a true beauty—bargain bin dress and uneven tan or no. She'd have looked spectacular wearing a paper bag. She glowed like a princess. *More than that*, Hadley had to admit.

"Fit for a bride," Karalee said, carefully tucking the veil back inside her bag. "Don't you think?"

Hadley nodded. *Fit for a queen*, she thought, her stomach twisting itself like a snake pinned to the ground by its head.

"I hope so. I sure do hope so." The gears of the Ferris wheel began cranking again, and their passenger car started its slow descent back to earth. "'Cuz, y'know," Karalee said softly, "I think it takes a long time to make things up to God."

On the car ride from the fairgrounds, Hadley said little and only half-listened to Ivy's tale of woe regarding her search for lodging. "Had to drive almost all the way to Bowling Green," her mother said, "to find somewhere decent people could stay." Hadley had no idea how far "all the way to Bowling Green" meant exactly, and wasn't sure if she even cared. She couldn't have felt more lost if her mother made her get out of the SUV and walk the rest of the way.

Now, standing in the bathroom and carefully removing her eyelash extensions and contact lenses, Hadley kept looking in the mirror. The image of Karalee was so clear in her mind, and yet try as hard as she could, she could find none of the other girl's beauty in her own reflection. *Beyond beauty*, she thought. *Majesty.* She tried to imagine holding the veil for herself (*silken*, she imagined, *of course it would be silken*) against her skin. But even in her daydream, she couldn't dare touch it. Her Congregationalist faith didn't generally lead her to think of objects in this manner, but the veil clearly came from someone—or something—higher than herself.

"Hadley!"

She jumped at the sound of her mother's voice.

"Yes, mother?"

"I've been talking to you for the last ten minutes," Ivy said from the other room, "and I don't think you've heard a single word."

"I'm just taking my face off," Hadley answered.

"So…what did you find out?"

Hadley froze for a second. *I found out I'm going to lose*, was her first thought.

Ivy appeared in the bathroom doorway. "What's with you?"

"Nothing."

"Please," Ivy began as she crossed her arms over her chest, "tell me you didn't spend three hours wandering around that bum-fuck fair like a dazed idiot."

Hadley's mind whirled. "Service," she blurted.

"What?"

"I met one of the other girls. She talked a lot about service. Made it seem important."

Ivy huffed. "Is that all?"

"No, but this girl made it seem really important." Hadley fought the urge to duck her mother's stare. *Make it a business deal*, she urged herself. *Make her buy what you're selling.* "Like there was nothing else even close to it," she finished.

A pause lingered, then Ivy was the one to drop her eyes. "You could make something out of that," she said. "Give me three synonyms for 'service.'"

"Duty," Hadley said. "Responsibility. Obligation."

"Good." Ivy turned away. "Repeat those ten times before you close your eyes tonight so they'll be deep in your head if they have you do an interview."

"Duty, responsibility, obligation," Hadley said for her mother's benefit. *Bullshit*, she added for herself. This was going to be a crash-and-burn of epic proportions, with a two-day drive back to Massachusetts for reliving the highlights. Hadley could see it coming as surely as if it had already happened. And then what?

Nothing—that's what. Her heart came untethered like a balloon escaping a child's reach. Suddenly it was clear to her what was worse than being a disappointment. She gripped the counter to hold herself steady. A disappointment still held a glimmer of hope, of possibility. Not that being a disappointment—and a perpetual one at that—was a desirable thing to be, but it was one rung higher than failure.

Failure. The word seemed to flash like neon across her face in the mirror. Right now, only she could see it. After tomorrow, everyone would.

"Mom?" Hadley called to the next room. *What do I do?* she wanted to ask.

"Don't forget your facial," Ivy yelled back. "You don't want a pizza-face for tomorrow, do you?"

Lying in bed, Hadley left her night mask down around her neck. Wearing it over her eyes, the darkness was so total she was scared it would swallow her. She tried to see through the blackness. Sophomore year was going to start in a month. Chemistry class with the dreaded Mr. Galley. Homecoming Dance in October.

None of it seemed to exist.

The heavy drapes were pulled over the windows and even if they weren't, the streetlamps in the parking lot would surely have bleached the stars out of the sky, and right now, Hadley wanted to see stars. *Star light, star bright*, she whispered to herself, *First star I see tonight…* Or the second, or the third. She'd wish on a billion—one at a time—if that's what it took. A wish for true beauty. A wish for majesty.

"Mother?" Her voice sounded so very loud in the stillness of the room.

"Mm," came the response from the next bed.

"Can we leave for the fair early in the morning?"

"Sure."

"Like, by five?"

Silence for a moment. "If you think it'll help."

Hadley closed her eyes and fell asleep more quickly than she thought she would. The next morning, as she awoke before the sun, she vaguely remembered dreaming about stars falling from the sky around her like rain. It felt like inspiration, which she took as a very good sign.

By the time Hadley and Ivy arrived back at the fairgrounds, Hadley realized that "inspiration" was really all that she had to go on. There wasn't a plan, or even an outline. She was stepping out onto a tightrope with no net and hard ground a long ways down. But what she did have was an image of herself standing on the opposite platform with a victorious smile. And that would have to be enough.

Ivy yawned loudly—an uncharacteristically un-ladylike bellow—as Hadley got out of the SUV with her garment bag and makeup case. "I suppose I have to drive all the way back now to find a Starbuck's."

"I'll be all right by myself." Hadley shut her door softly and walked toward the main gate with the crunch of the Escalade's tires through the gravel crackling in her ears. This early in the day, even if it was the day of the pageant, she was surprised (but pleased) to find the ticket booth unattended. Hadley walked through the generous gap in the sliding gate. *This is how it will happen*, she thought. *One piece after another falling automatically into place.* The whole puzzle would've been too intricate for her to figure out ahead of time. If things were going to happen for her, they were going to happen spontaneously. As a matter of…inspiration.

She walked up one row of booths, then started to cut across an open lawn between her and the central tent where all the "Daughters of Holden Hill" would gather. She took a couple of step on the grass, then stopped. The expanse was covered with a hundred, maybe a couple hundred, dew-covered spider-webs glistening as the first rays of sunlight began to seep into the valley. They were all funnel-shaped, tapering down through the grass. From the side, they looked like wispy tornadoes, frozen in time. Hadley found herself stepping around them as best she could. They reminded her of spun glass, and she even thought she heard a gentle tinkling from them every time she took a step.

She had reached the middle of the lawn when another thought crossed her mind. Webs kissed by morning dew might look pretty, but they had a real purpose. Webs were meant to catch food. And if each of these had its designer sitting within, just out of sight…and then if all those spiders sensed her presence and decided to come out at the same time…

A soft sound, like the ripping of a fine cloth, floated up from behind her.

Hadley ran, zig-zagging between the webs—only they didn't seem like webs anymore, but mouths lying in wait for something to bite, to catch, to tear. Her heart leapt into her throat every time she had to put her foot down, for fear something on the ground would grab it.

At last, she reached the tent and slipped inside a side flap. The first thing she did was look at the ground. Dirt. Runners of black plastic criss-crossing in front of a three-foot tall wooden stage made the ground look like a checkerboard. But no grass, and no webs. *Our imagination is getting a little frisky, isn't it?* she chided herself. And indeed, the way that the nighttime gloom seemed to cling stubbornly despite the rising light of day made her feel as if she were inside some kind of dream. *Anxiety from a guilty conscience?* Hadley wondered. Ridiculous. She hadn't done anything yet. Except that she had. In her heart, in her head—even in her soul—she had already done things to feel guilty for. Her future was already a past just waiting to happen.

She looked around. Empty—still no one else to see. She headed around the stage and to the curtained area behind it. A row of desks and chairs—borrowed from the local school, perhaps—filled the back. Cheap door mirrors turned lengthwise leaned precariously across the desks. At either end of the row stood empty clothing racks and tri-fold screens forming closet-sized changing areas.

Hadley put her things behind the screen closest to her. That was the place to wait. If someone came in—the wrong someone—it would still be all right. The new girl was just early. *That's all there is to it*, she thought. Wait and see who came in next.

The hour was still early, as it so happened, when Hadley heard Fate coming for her. The sun had risen past the hilltops, bringing golden light through the seams of the tent flaps and down through the mesh netting high above. Hadley listened intently to the sounds of footsteps coming around the stage out front, then back towards the dressing area. She held her breath as she dared to peek around the screen.

There was Karalee, alone, seated at the closest desk, looking freshly cleaned and hair brushed although wearing the same dress as yesterday. And carrying the same canvas shoulder bag. Hadley's eyes twinkled. The veil was in there—she didn't have to see it to know it was true. Now all she needed was the opportunity. Fifteen seconds alone with the bag. Maybe less. Everything else had worked out so far, now she just needed one last roll of the dice to go her way.

Step outside, step outside! Hadley tried to beam the suggestion into Karalee's head. But instead, Karalee positioned herself for the perfect view of herself in the mirror, then reached into her bag. She removed the veil and as if on cue, a ray of sunlight caught it. The flow of time slipped into slow-motion. Each little sparkle stretched lazily across the seconds, and Hadley drank in every bit of its beauty. *Fit for a queen*, she thought. *Fit for a queen, fit for a—*

"Hadley?"

Hadley gasped. She felt like the tiny ball on the roulette wheel—one instant skipping and spinning, and then suddenly grabbed out of mid-air. She didn't remember coming out from behind the screen, or stepping forward until she was standing directly behind Karalee's chair. And yet, there she was. Out in the open.

"Hadley?" Karalee asked again. The girls' eyes met in the mirror.

"What?"

Hadley looked in Karalee's lap. The stupid girl was bunching the veil, twisting it in her hands. The blood surged in her veins. *It's not a dish rag!* she shouted inside her head. Her cheeks got warm, and a reddish haze came over her eyes. *Not a dish rag! Not a dish rag!*

Karalee started to turn around and as she did, the wooden chair made a sharp creaking sound that Hadley heard as if it were a rifle shot zipping past her head. Her body reacted on its own, without waiting for any conscious instruction. She'd never made a fist before in her life, but suddenly there was one at the end of both her arms and she swung them like wrecking balls. Both caught Karalee in the face—one in the middle of her forehead and the other in her mouth—and sent her sprawling out of her chair and into the one next to it.

She hadn't even finished falling before Hadley was on top of her. "Dish rag, dish rag, dish rag," she repeated in a voice that was hot and cool all at the same time. Her hands were wrapped all the way around Karalee's neck and working the windpipe as if she were trying to wring the other girl dry. Karalee's eyes bulged. She kicked uselessly and tried to tear into Hadley's hands to make her let go. Maybe she even did, but Hadley didn't feel it. She kept squeezing and watching how Karalee's eyes were losing their focus. Red cracks, like fault lines, split through the whites. The light in her irises grew dimmer…and dimmer…and went out.

When Hadley's body relinquished control and her mind could again process what had happened, Karalee's body was dead weight in her hands. She released her grip and stared for a moment at the purplish bruising around Karalee's neck, trying to figure out how that could have happened.

The veil!

Hadley looked behind her. There it was, lying in the dirt next to the first overturned chair. She carefully lifted it up, holding it to the light. Not a rip, nor even a wrinkle. It wasn't even smudged.

Carefully, Hadley folded the veil and put it in her own handbag behind the tri-fold. She was considerably less graceful with Karalee—grabbing the body by the wrists and dragging it out of the dressing area to the back of the stage. Red, white, and blue bunting decorated the platform on three sides, but the rear section was open. Hadley pulled, pushed, and rolled Karalee until she was far enough forward to be obscured by the shadows from anyone casually walking around the back.

When she got back behind the curtains, her mind began to whirl with one urgent issue after another. *What about Karalee's bag?* Drop it in a dumpster. *You look a mess from crawling under that stage.* Wash face and hands in the main pavilion restroom, then change clothes. *Your hands!* Karalee had scratched her up pretty good. *I have white gloves*, Hadley thought. *Might be nice, give myself a Jackie O. look.* And one last thing—don't be the first to arrive. Walk around, hang out on the fringes until later. Even better, get outside the gates and come back in. No one will ever know.

She gripped her handbag in her hands almost as tightly as she had Karalee's neck. *Don't let this out of your hands!* She felt a powerful need to look inside. What if the treasure had fallen out somehow? What if someone else took it while she was hiding Karalee?

She opened the handbag. It was still there.

Hadley slipped out the side of the pageant tent and ran for the cover of the shrouded booths. With their flaps tied down, they all looked like canvas mausoleums. From somewhere—near the front gates—she thought she heard a car or truck pull in to the parking lot, the engine rattling to a halt. *Go the long way around*, she thought. *Restroom, then out the back of the fairgrounds and around in through the front again.*

As she came around the corner of one of the booths, Hadley suddenly stopped in her racks. A spider stood directly in her path—the body alone as big as a tea-cup. Long, bristling black-and-brown hair covered its legs and torso. Two hours ago, the sight of it would've made her scream. Now, she lifted her foot over it. Like Karalee said on the

Ferris wheel—*no big deal.* Just a crawly-thing about to become a stain on the bottom of her shoe.

Then the spider suddenly reared up, lifting half its legs in the air and waving them at her in a warning. Hadley suddenly had an image in her head from the spider's point-of-view, and the strength of its defiance made her feel taller, somehow, more mighty.

More royal.

She moved her own foot back and set it down. "All right," she said approvingly. "You get to live."

Slowly, she began backing up, waiting for the spider to acknowledge that the threat had passed. But it didn't. It stayed rock-still and ready to fight even as Hadley retreated farther and farther away. She felt its eyes on her, as she had on the picnic table and up in the Ferris wheel, and there was a good thirty feet between them before she felt safe turning away.

And even then, as she wandered past the booths and the animal pavilions, Hadley kept turning around every so often to look on the ground behind her.

"A fine day," Hadley heard Collins say as she stood backstage, just out of view of the audience.

"Yes," Mr. Cahill agreed. "God be thanked for it."

"Of course, of course."

Hadley watched Collins bow his head slightly and shuffle his feet, like a little boy being reminded of his manners. His reaction was pretty much identical to the energy Hadley had been sensing all morning from the crowds. Everyone seemed to have a squirming kind of excitement they were trying to keep bottled inside. They were like kids sitting through a sunrise service on Christmas Day.

Some of that tension was also due to Karalee's absence. An older man, with similar-looking eyes and nose, came in and went out again a couple of times. *Her dad*, Hadley guessed. From what she could pick up from snippets of conversations, a girl dropping out suddenly was not unheard of, but it apparently meant she was never going to be seen again. She wouldn't have dared to take on that much shame.

At least, that's as much as Hadley was able to put together. The other girls in the pageant—about a dozen—whispered around her, but no one spoke to her directly. They accepted her presence because she had the white ribbon, but otherwise she was a stranger and (as Hadley remembered Karalee's reactions from the night before) an exotic stranger at that. If she'd walked into their midst with a green mohawk and studded leather jacket instead of her Trina Turk dress, she could not have stood apart any more. And so she was left with the enormity of what she'd done sitting on her heart as if she was on the bottom of the ocean, looking up to see only a faint glow where there used to be the sun, and warmth, and fresh air.

But then she would lightly finger the veil—folded immaculately into a pocket square—between her palms, and its luxurious touch melted her anxieties away. *Fit for a queen*, she told herself, and the image of a crown atop her head (*and not one of those plastic tiaras, but a full-fledged, twice-as-big-as-her-head crown*) brought back the glow to her cheeks and the shine to her eyes.

On a few occasions, Mr. Cahill ushered some older men through— each one dressed in a white shirt and either a brown or blue suit. Their presence might have seemed inappropriate amidst teenage girls in a dressing area, except that Hadley was the only one to have even brought a change of clothes. There was the tuxedo-style halter dress she had on, plus a strapless cotton sun dress and a black sequin mini that went with the Donna Karan heels which practically lifted her ass up to the small of her back. The others simply had what they were wearing when they arrived—plain dresses from straight off the rack—and yet they received the same stares and murmured commentary that Hadley got.

Amazingly, her mother had not appeared backstage, which was a mixed blessing. Hadley didn't have the pressure of Miss Massachusetts leaning over her shoulder, but neither did she have any reconnaissance. She hadn't seen any schedule of events, or program listings, or anything. Whenever she could find someone to ask about the judging, the only answers she got were variations on "Soon" and "They'll know it when they see it".

Shortly after a noon fire whistle had gone off to mark the hour (which Hadley momentarily took as an alarm that Karalee's body had been found), Collins arrived to gather the girls together. He counted heads and led them to where they were standing now—in front of steps leading up to the stage. On the opposite side, Mr. Cahill wheeled Anna up a ramp. She had on a new white dress to go with her faded ribbon, and a crown on her head that looked (Hadley appraised sadly) like plastic. Mr. Cahill set her in place and locked down her chair before joining Collins near the contestants. They both looked out and seemed to be waiting for something, while making occasional quiet remarks to each other that Hadley couldn't catch.

From what she could hear of the audience, however, it sounded like it was growing steadily larger. The sounds of their conversations went from a hum to a buzz to a soft rumbling, like distant thunder. It was at this point that Mr. Cahill strode away from Collins and headed for the microphone center-stage. The crowd settled itself well before he reached his destination, and even the noises outside hushed themselves as if a sign of silence had been passed from one end of the fairgrounds to the other. The only thing to be heard was the whirring of the ventilation fans up above.

"Brothers and Sisters!" Mr. Cahill began. Hadley imagined she heard the sound of a few hundred heads bowing simultaneously. "Sons and Daughters of Holden Hill! On the final day of our Covenant, we pray for renewal. Just as the rains nourish the fields, and the fields nourish the flock, and the flock nourishes the shepherd. Praise the day."

"Praise the day," the crowd repeated.

"As it was long ago, we remember it today. As our fathers and grandfathers had seen it, we see it now. The Eve of our Destruction. The sky as black as coal, and the air filled with a roar, and the ground falling away from our feet—oh, praise the day!"

"Praise the day!" the crowd replied.

"And we cry out to be saved, and we beg for one more dawn, and the Great One said, What will you give? A dawn cannot be bought with silver, or built with sweat. And the people answer: Life! Life begets Life! Praise the day!"

"Amen!" some called out from the crowd. "Praise the day!"

"For seven times seven years, we now pray for renewal," Mr. Cahill said, raising his voice just enough to regain the audience's attention. "Let Life beget Life!"

Hadley leaned around the girls in front of her to glimpse Anna in her chair, propped up like a grotesque Halloween lawn decoration. Her eyes were open, but blank. The only sign of life was a twitch in her hands, folded over her balloon-belly. Tiny spasms of her fingers, almost as if she were secretly conducting an invisible orchestra. *Seven years?* Hadley thought. *What do they do to you down here for seven years to turn you into that?*

Just then, Collins began motioning for the line of girls to come up on stage. Hadley watched the three in front of her climb the steps and then walk in single file to the far end. The one immediately before her (*Nora*, Hadley thought was her name) was trembling so much she nearly shook herself off the top step. *That'll cost you points*, she thought instinctively.

Now Collins was waving for her to come on, and as Hadley put her foot on the first step, she could see just enough of the audience waiting for her to spot the Suits now standing front and center. Her mother was just behind them, video camera doubtlessly zoomed in on the spot where Hadley was about to appear. *This is it*, she realized, and another little voice inside her head (she dared to call it *Inspiration*) confirmed that she was right. She felt the stares fall upon her skin, her hair, her dress. And not just the stares of these judges and this audience, but everyone from all the pageants, and the talent competitions, and the school dances, and the school hallways. They were waiting for the Golden Girl to shine, and here was the Last Hope, the Last Chance to catch fire or else dwindle and wink out forever.

As Hadley reached the top step, she made a sweeping gesture with her right arm and cast the folded veil out in front and above her, like serving on a tennis court. *One chance—either gonna work, or it's not.* But it did work, and work to perfection. The gossamer square arced out in front of her and unfolded itself like a parachute, now gently descending, catching the light on its way down and sparkling even more in this moment than Hadley had ever seen before.

As she stepped onto the stage, the veil settled perfectly over her head and shoulders. A collective "Ohhh!" arose from the crowd followed by a roar of cheers. Hadley couldn't see very well to either side, but she could imagine the look on her mother's face, her jaw dropped open. She smiled from ear to ear. The moment was magical; it was divine.

It was Inspirational.

Mr. Cahill intercepted her before she could take three more steps. He took both her hands in his and gazed deeply into her eyes through the veil. His mouth worked open and closed as if he were trying to speak but was too overcome to make the words come out. *Holy shit*, Hadley thought, *is he crying?* He led her to the center of the stage and tenderly lifted the veil back from her face. Then, he turned to the crowd and in a booming voice (even without benefit of the microphone) announced: "The Queen has been chosen! The Covenant is renewed!"

Another roar erupted, even louder than the first. Joy swept toward Hadley in a wave, broke overhead, and showered her. And her mother—Ivy was leaping up and down, waving madly with the camera still in the palm of one hand, but for all intents and purposes pretty much forgotten.

Mr. Cahill leaned close to speak in Hadley's ear. "I didn't know if it could be you, but you did it! You were the One!"

Suddenly, Hadley was surrounded by the Suits and a grand chair was brought in behind her. *My throne*, she thought. She glanced over to where Anna was sitting and saw Collins easing the tiara off of her head. Somehow it didn't look so cheap anymore. *For me*, Hadley thought. *For the Queen.*

As Collins handed the tiara to Mr. Cahill, Anna suddenly pitched forward in her chair, then snapped back again as if her spine had frozen into a straight line. Her eyes gaped open so wide they seemed to take over half her face, and she emitted a scream that crashed through the celebration like a rock through plate glass. The crowd was stunned into silence for a moment.

"Praise the day!" someone shouted, and a hundred more echoed back the words. Three of the Suits ran to Anna's side, who was now screeching and thrashing like a wild animal. They lifted her from the wheelchair and laid her on the stage. Hadley started to rise from her seat too, but Mr. Cahill moved in her way.

"Sit, please," he said, and two other Suits guided her back to her throne by her arms.

"Oh my God," Hadley said, "call a doctor!"

"It's all right," Mr. Cahill said, circling around the back of Hadley's chair with the tiara held aloft for all to see. "It's a blessed moment when a Daughter becomes a Bride."

Anna's cries drew Hadley's attention again. Three men were holding her down, but even so it looked like she was about to throw them off at any moment. Then, all at once, she stopped—her back arched and her belly pushed high into the air. The audience was silent, holding their breaths along with her, until Anna found a whole new pitch and volume for her screams. A red stain began seeping through her dress across her belly. The sound of wet meat being ripped from the bone filled the air. One of the Suits leaned forward and tore Anna's dress down the middle. Her belly had split open. Dozens of black spiders— each one as big as a golf ball—were clambering over one another, slipping in the crimson and grey juices as they escaped her ruptured womb.

"Glory to the Covenant!" shouted the crowd. "Praise the day!"

Hadley's mouth went dry. The air seemed to vanish from around her, making it impossible for her to cry or call out. "A Bride?" she squeaked.

"And also a blessed moment," Mr. Cahill said, lowering the tiara onto Hadley's brow, "when a Bride becomes a Mother."

The words struck Hadley like fists. At first, all she could do was stare at the crowd. Some were praying, some were laughing, many were weeping with ecstasy. The one bit of screaming she heard she knew was coming from her mother. *The Daughter becomes the Bride, becomes the Mother*, Hadley thought, with her plastic crown and spider-web trousseau. *Life begets life.* She could see it all for herself, her future no longer the emptiness she'd glimpsed the night before. And while she knew that, one day, there would be a time for screaming, right now there was love, and laughter, and tears of joy. All as it should be, when a crowd was in the presence of a queen.

I did it, Mother. I'm the Queen, she thought. *I'm the Queen, I'm the Queen, I'm the...*

Leave 'em Laughing

Becca Farrell was squeezing me too tight.

Normally I wouldn't have considered this a problem. Her body curved perfectly into mine, her breasts rubbing me up and down as she gasped for breath in short, sharp heaves. But then on a normal Friday night (early Saturday morning, technically speaking) I wouldn't be hiding in a janitor's closet. I don't know how long we had been in there. Long enough for it to seem safe, even though she was still whimpering. The only thing I could think to do was pull her close and muffle her voice against my shoulder, but within a few minutes the pins-and-needles sensation in my arms had gone from itch to burn. When I tried to adjust my hold, she whined and suddenly clutched—squeezing the air out of me like a bagpipe.

"Jesus!" I said. "Let me go for five seconds."

She moaned but did, indeed, relax her grip while still basically clinging to me. I moved her a bit more so I could turn to face the door.

"Don't!"

"I'm just trying to get to my cell phone." I pivoted carefully, trying to keep my elbows from bumping into the mops and brooms hanging on the walls around us. I also didn't want to fumble and drop the phone while pulling it out of my jeans—there'd be no way to bend over and pick it up unless one of us was a contortionist. Ultimately it didn't matter. Whether it was the junction box in the closet with us or the exposed

I-beam, I had only one signal bar blinking on and off. Mostly off. I wasn't going to get out even a text or a tweet, much less a phone call.

I started to reach for the doorknob. Becca's fingernails dug into my shoulders even through my shirt. "He… he… he…"

Oh Christ, I thought, *she's gone.* And she wasn't a Rhodes Scholar to begin with.

"He's not out there," I said.

"You don't know, you don't know—"

And that was certainly true. I didn't have x-ray vision, but I didn't hear anything. No footsteps, no shouts, no laughing.

I was especially happy not to hear that laughing.

All of which meant Gary was not waiting for us right outside the door. But the more rational that conclusion seemed, the more I mistrusted it because—rationally—Becca and I shouldn't be hiding in a closet in the first place because—rationally—Gary should not have split open Matt's face with the blade arm of a paper-cutter.

…not just his face, but his whole fucking skull. One moment Gary suddenly appeared in the doorway, and the next Matt's eyes were bulging like a frog's on either side of the blade. Blood and brains dripped down his face like melted ice-cream, soaking into his scraggly beard. And Gary was still laughing—that full-throated bellowing laugh—as he pulled on the handle, working to dislodge his weapon from his friend's face.

The sudden memory had me frozen in place—hand resting on the doorknob, Becca practically crawling up my back, sweat rolling into my eyes, and the strong possibility that a dude I'd just met was outside waiting to take a hack at us. Actually, that much I could sorta handle. Not that I usually provoke murderous rages, but I've said the wrong thing to the wrong guy before. I've been slapped, and knocked to the floor, and the small scar above my right eye is from a beer bottle flung at me from across the room. I've seen people lose their temper, but never their mind. Not all at once, anyway. Not right there in front of me.

I mean, Friday nights were made for other things. That's why I was following Becca around in the first place. We'd hooked up on Bell Street along a block of wall-to-wall bars where the townies drive by shouting insults at the guys and pick-up lines to the girls. After we'd hit a couple different spots I thought we were ready to settle in for the night, if you know what I mean. Becca was into the thrill of the chase, though. She wanted to go to the campus radio station because the midnight-to-3 a.m. deejay was someone she'd gone to high school with.

What the hell, I thought. It was too late to ditch her and try for someone else and I figured it was still about 70/30 that the night would end in a tangle in one of our dorm rooms. So we went in the Speech and Communications building, down into the basement where I met Matt. Nice guy. In fact, on first impression I liked him a lot because he looked like a living stick-figure. No body fat, but no muscle either. The burliest thing about him was his beard running wild across his face like an old hedge. Definitely not competition.

However, the other guy—Matt's roommate—made me worry.

This was Gary, and Becca's head turned so fast that I felt the breeze. Average height, average build, but with dark hair and dark skin—the kind that always looks tanned no matter what the season. He didn't talk much, but his eyes made you think he was listening intently to everything being said. That's what concerned me most. Girls love listeners.

Anyway, Gary was there because the station had a room of old vinyl LPs and he was supposed to go through and figure out if any were worth keeping. Sounded like as much fun as going to the flea market with my Aunt Deb, but Becca decided she wanted to help out for a while. Of course, Gary did also have a bottle of Jameson's and was offering shots to anyone who found something cool. Becca wasn't one to pass up free whiskey and frankly, neither was I.

So we settled in among the stacks of wax, with Matt drifting in and out between cuing sets on his show. I knew, even having been bribed with spirits, that we were in for a lot of shit-work. A university radio station is a dumping ground for demo records and bands whose chief claims to fame include the county fair circuit. Lots of crap to sort through and furthermore, it became quickly obvious that my "date" didn't know Iggy Pop from Ziggy Stardust. But any interesting album cover was a good enough excuse to run over and show Gary what she'd just found. I couldn't tell who she was really playing with—me or him.

Sometimes a girl who otherwise doesn't have much upstairs can be a level-twelve grandmaster in the mindgames of Mating and Dating.

Just when I was most desperately needing to draw an ace, I found an album tucked behind one of the shelves I knew was gonna be good for a distraction. Front and back were covered with a red-and-black diamond pattern, like a cartoon court jester's outfit. Across the top was (I assumed) the band's name: Zanni.

Yeah, I thought at first. *Zanni-zany, lame-lamey.* But just as the album was about to land in the trash pile, a small label in the bottom corner of the flip side caught my eye. In tiny print it read: "PARENTS: Do not allow unsupervised minors to play the last track of side B backwards."

I laughed. No teenager in 1978 (or whenever this band was around) could resist buying the record solely for the purpose of rushing home and doing exactly what the label told them not to. And the same psychology also worked on my new friend, Gary. Once I showed it to him—and collected my shot of Jameson's—he led the way into a smaller studio where they still had a turntable hooked up. He put the needle on the last track and started winding the record counter-clockwise. Now, I'm not sure what I was expecting. Sparks flying, or a deep voice reciting Satanic incantations. At the very least, I was hoping for some new and exciting swear words. But all that came out of the speakers were warped guitars and drums. Which was funny to listen to.

For about three seconds.

Swing and a miss, I thought.

But while Becca, Matt and I were cracking jokes about "scary side B", Gary was hunkered over the turntable. He reset the needle and wound the record around and around over and over again.

"You guys shut up!"

"What?" I said.

"Trying to listen."

I looked at Becca and Matt, who both shrugged. "Dude, there's nothing there. The label was bullshitting us."

Gary got up from his chair to grab a set of headphones. "I can almost hear it."

Suddenly my swinging strike had turned into extra bases.

With Gary plugged into the turntable, I was the most interesting male in the room again. Plus, the Jameson's was now completely unguarded. Matt hurried back to his booth to do a station i.d. break while Becca and I returned to the storeroom. We sat cross-legged on the floor side by side, her knee resting on top of mine, and helped ourselves to a series of shots.

After toasting the health and wealth of several bands neither one of us had ever heard of, she leaned back on her elbows. "Aren't you going to kiss me?" she asked.

The next thing I knew, Matt was discreetly knocking on the open door and telling us it was time to lock up. His show was over, the station had signed off for the night, and none of us had seen Gary for almost an hour.

When we looked into the little studio, Gary was still sitting in the same chair, headphones on, bent over the turntable. He was shaking—shoulders bobbing up and down like he was quietly laughing at the funniest joke he'd ever heard in his life. Matt tapped him on the shoulder and when Gary whirled around, I actually jumped. His face and shirt collar were soaked—from sweat or tears, I couldn't tell. He started scream-laughing right in Matt's face, and when he saw Becca and me in the doorway, that was even funnier. We all waited for him to take a breath so we could ask what was going on, but he never did. He just stood, removed the 'phones, and walked past us into the studio office down the hallway. As he went by, I could hear him making sharp, hoarse gasps—kinda like my sister's cat dry-heaving right before yakking on the carpet.

We all stared, waiting to see which of us was gonna come up with an explanation, when we heard a cracking sound—which now I know was Gary breaking off the arm of the paper-cutter they once used to cut-and-paste news items from the old AP teletype.

Matt started moving first, leaving Becca and me a few paces behind. "Gary, what the fuck…?" he said just before reaching the doorway and meeting the paper-cutter blade with his face.

What the fuck, indeed.

Becca took off running and I followed her because I'd never been down in the radio station before. But she was screaming and crying the whole time, and obviously had no idea where she was going either. Every office and studio had at least three doors and were clustered inside a narrow hallway wrapping around all four sides. To get off the floor, there were stairwell exits on either end, but whichever one we headed for, Gary got there first like Pepé Le Pew chasing his French pussy. One minute he was behind us, so we'd duck into one room and out through another to get back to the hallway and suddenly that screaming laugh would burst out from exactly the direction we wanted to go.

We ran in circles—doubling back on our double-backs—for what felt like forever before finally getting a clear shot at an exit. Once in the stairwell, I took the steps two at a time to get up to the outside door. I leaned forward to smash the panic bar with all my momentum and pop it open—

—and the door said, *Fuck you*. The only thing that popped was my shoulder. I stared at the door trying to figure out what was wrong. I could understand doors being locked after hours to keep people from getting in, but how could it be locked to keep people from getting out? I pushed on it again. It didn't budge. My face got hot. I heard someone laughing, but this wasn't funny. It was wrong, it wasn't fucking fair!

Becca grabbed me by my arm and started tugging me up to the next landing. Every door was locked until, finally, the one on the fourth floor let us through. I had the thought that we were being herded, but the need to escape through any available opening was far too strong to overcome. We tried two classroom doors before Becca found the janitor's closet with the wiring and exposed steel that ruined my cell phone reception.

I felt like I'd been standing there at the door for an hour. The knob was starting to feel warm from holding it so long. *There's no one there*, I told myself. *No one there, no one there, no one there …*

I eased the door open. As soon as there was a crack of light through the doorway, the phone in my hand suddenly buzzed. I almost dropped the stupid thing.

"Help, help, help!" Becca squeaked.

"It's a text, dummy!" I hissed at her.

"What's it say?"

I pushed the "OK" button to open the message and my gut twisted so hard I thought I was going to throw up.

It said, "Knock, knock."

The door flew open out of my hands. I had a flash of Gary's arm rocketing toward me. He grabbed the front of my shirt (he practically grabbed me by my skin!) and yanked me off my feet. I went flying over his shoulder, but only as far as the opposite wall. I managed to curl and cover fast enough to keep from meeting the concrete with my face, but even still I hit hard enough to make fireworks go off in my head.

Gary looked down at me, laughing. Laughing so hard that tears of blood slid from the corners of his eyes, leaving pinkish streaks down his cheeks and chin. He winked at me as if to say, *Hang tight, you're gonna love this!* And then he stepped into the closet.

The screams were not human. My brain first tried, then refused, to imagine what could cause such sounds. They meant death, of course, but before that, a fifty-foot plunge into insanity. I heard—between the wails and the giggles—wet, ripping noises like the tearing of limbs around a Thanksgiving table. Agony, in its purest and most primal form, popped the balloon holding Becca's mind together as her cries turned into drowning gurgles, and then a terrible, empty silence.

I laid on the floor right where I'd fallen when I should have been running, but I had absolutely shut down. Time had frozen, and then skipped forward to Gary leaving the closet, the whole front of him soaked in hues of red from scarlet to almost black. Glops of… something… fell off his hands. I tried to get to my feet. At least, I gave the order to stand. But my body was fatally slow to react. Gary wrapped his hands around my neck and lifted me in the air while my arms and legs flailed uselessly.

I thought I was finished. It was just a question of what was going to give first—my windpipe or my whole fucking neck. But after a couple of seconds, I realized I wasn't dead yet. A feeling like lightning shot through my veins, spinning me backwards from acceptance into anger. My mind and body snapped into alignment again—no more haze, no more time-delay. As soon as I had the idea, my leg pulled back and I kicked Gary in the balls. He didn't stop laughing, but his eyes got really big and the grip around my neck loosened just a little.

Instinctively I kicked again, and if I'd made solid contact before, then this time I went *through* him. I could've made a 55-yard field goal at Lambeau Field with that kick. Against the wind. Gary dropped me and folded in half. I sucked in a full breath of air, which was like dry-swallowing thumbtacks, but I didn't let that slow me down. While I hadn't planned this far ahead, I knew I had one chance to get the upper hand. I got in behind him, wrapping one arm around his neck and squeezing as hard as I could. After being thrown around once already, I knew he was stronger than he had any right to be, but with the crook of my elbow under his chin I was betting that my leverage would beat his muscles.

Gary straightened and tried to reach around to grab me, but he couldn't get hold of anything. He grabbed at my arm to pull me off, digging his fingers into my flesh. Part of me wanted to warn him—tell him that the more he struggled the more he was going to get hurt. But I swallowed those words thinking about Matt and Becca, and where he had me just a minute ago. In fact, I started considering twisting his damn head off like a bottle cap.

Then I noticed he wasn't laughing any more. Actually, it was a bigger difference than that. When I'd first grabbed him, it was like jumping on the back of a tornado. But now the storm had broken, blown itself out. The way he beat at my arms wasn't angry. He wasn't fighting back, just trying to tap out. I relaxed a bit and it was his turn to gulp a little air.

"Please…" he croaked.

"Shut up, man." I didn't want to let go until he was unconscious, which I thought should've happened by now. Sixty seconds ago, I was ready to kill. But now the adrenaline rush was subsiding, handing control back over to the logical side of my brain, which promptly began to deny the reality of the last hour or so.

Gary coughed. "You gotta… you gotta…"

"Shut up!" I tried to sound angry and then feel as angry as I sounded because a soft numb feeling was creeping up from the back of my skull. Some kind of late-night watchman was turning me off one switch at a time. *Poor bastard*, he was thinking. *This is more than he can handle. Better shut down.*

"Gotta... gotta..."

"Gotta what?" I yelled, shaking Gary but really shaking myself. "Huh? Gotta what?"

"Gotta... hear this one. It'll kill ya!"

Nothing he said made sense at first, no more than the noises off the record. But it wasn't the words anyway. It was the *sounds* of the words making Gary laugh as he talked. But even then, it wasn't at all like before. This laughter was ten thousand ice needles digging under my skull. It picked at my mind, like digging at a scab. I felt myself being peeled open, cold air blowing across the wet, pulpy sponge of my brain. A hundred new senses and a thousand new sensations blasted through me. I could smell pain like a perfume, hear Gary's heart thundering in my ears. And more. It wasn't a taste or an odor, but I could sense his soul, too. I suddenly knew everything about him. Joys, losses, hopes, fears—they all flooded through me. They tickled (*heh*). Holding him this close to me was like there being no difference between us at all. Only the flesh (*heh, heh*) kept us apart.

The sensations of both his soul and mine surged like a sun blazing before exploding. I was going to go nova right there unless...

I opened my mouth and let out a long laugh. Felt good. Felt fucking fantastic, so I did it again. And my laugh was making Gary laugh. He didn't have any air to laugh with, but still I heard it. I tightened my grip, squeezing his head like an orange. He was still laughing. I was still laughing.

When I let Gary go, his face had gone white. Eyes stared wide open at nothing, filled with red cracks. He looked funny. I wiped away tears running down my face, the blood staining my fingers. *If he could see himself now...*

I packed him in with Becca inside the janitor's closet, then swabbed the hallway floor with bleach. My skin kept tingling the whole time and I started thinking that everybody could feel this amazing sensation if only they could wake up to it. Have the dull mucus sucked off their minds and let them feel what I was feeling. But first I'd have to get them loose. I could dress for the occasion—get a red-and-black diamond outfit from the Theatre/Dance Department. Then go find a party on Sorority Row. Make the girls split a gut, have a howl. Leave 'em laughing.

After all, if there's anyone who enjoys a good laugh, it's sorority girls.

Rapture

His arms swung round like a Pete Townshend windmill, smashing out the chord. Vibrations ran through his body—first as a tingling, then a burning, then a shredding sensation as if glass shards were swimming through his veins…

A hole opened through the fog of sleep and vodka. Just a pinprick at first, then gradually widening as Gideon opened his eyes and began to take in the familiar shapes of his apartment—the battered box fan propped in the window, the stack of plastic milk-crates in the corner containing vaguely organized piles of t-shirts, socks, and underwear. The music from the dream began to fade, drowning in the static of his waking mind. It didn't sound familiar—certainly not part of the set he'd played earlier tonight—but not totally unfamiliar, either. Like a song he'd once heard but never paid attention to. Now it was stuck in his subconscious, scratching at him from a place he couldn't reach.

He slipped quietly off the mattress, trying not to disturb the woman slumbering on the other side. She stirred momentarily under the sheet, undraping one perfect pillowy breast. *Caron*, he remembered. *With a "c".* She'd written her name and number on a scrap of sheet music from his guitar case—not that it had been necessary. Their bodies had been glued together from the club to his bed, and yet staring at her now, he struggled to recall what is was like to hold her. Like she was part of a dream that had followed him into the waking world. Nothing was wrong that he could identify, but something about her being here didn't make sense—like reading the face of a clock but not understanding what the numbers meant.

The meds were probably doing that to him. Last month, the clinic docs had changed his prescription because the old stuff started making him want to claw his skin to ribbons every other night. The new tabs were just as extreme, but on the other end of the spectrum—not much different than wrapping himself in thick plastic. While he could still find the chords to play, the sound fell dead two seconds after leaving the strings. He wasn't the second coming of Hendrix or anything—his "career" was about cover songs and tribute bands—but he still needed to feel the music flowing through. If that meant playing with a looser grip on reality than normal, so be it.

He bent over the crumpled heap of his jeans, fumbling through the pockets until he found his last pack and his last cigarette. The air in the apartment hung wet and heavy but as he shuffled towards his kitchen, a teasing hint of a breeze beckoned through the window screen. Gideon kicked back in a vinyl chair and lit up. He was pretty sure half a bottle of Smirnoff waited in the back of the refrigerator freezer if he had trouble going back to sleep later. *Get tight, get loose*, he thought. *Everybody needs a routine.*

His eyes began to adjust to the nighttime gloom and he frowned as he spied the outline of the Stratocaster case sitting just inside the back door. Hot sex or not, he should've put it away in his bedroom, not left it with only a mesh screen to keep out any asshole who wanted a free guitar. He pulled the case onto the table and flipped open the latches. The instrument gleamed inside, catching a bit of the shine from the streetlights. His first thought was that he was too tired to mess with anything now. But it seemed to want to be held. Already he could feel the tingling sensations of the strings singing into the pads of his fingers. *Why not?* he thought.

A streak of sheet lightning filled the sky just as Gideon stepped onto the fire escape, hefting the guitar and an old home-stereo speaker to use as an amp. Sweat trickled down the back of his neck almost immediately as he settled on the top step. The asphalt and concrete below had spent all day soaking in the sun and even now, in the last hours of night, were still releasing their heat back into the air. Gideon laid his cigarette on the step, set his fingers to the Strat, and let his conscious mind float off to the side. The song which had stirred him from sleep danced on the edge of his senses, skipping away again whenever it was about to come in clearly. He resisted the temptation to chase after it, waiting instead for the music to come to him. At first, the guitar just made noise. But he kept playing, purposely not paying attention to what he was strumming.

Emptying his mind to catch the song rattling around in there left an opening for odd memories to bubble to the surface. For whatever reason, he remembered one time waking up on the floor of his bedroom and rolling over into a puddle of fermented vomit. Next came an image from the rehab: lifting his head and thinking that when he looked in the bathroom mirror, he would see his skin bubbling and popping. In truth, the image revealed to him then had been even worse. He had the look of a man dead for two weeks: bulging frog-like eyes as listless as smoky marbles, grey and puffy skin sagging off his face like wet meat.

Gideon pushed all those memories through his fingers, then out the guitar until they began to distance and die. Playing through the memories changed something, but he couldn't tell what. It was the same technique he always used, but he was reaching further with it than ever before—beyond just hearing the music, beyond the vibrations in his hands. He almost felt outside his own body, and the rush was electric.

He continued to play even as the door opened behind him and Caron stepped outside. She had pulled on her shirt and jean shorts and made a place for herself leaning against the brick façade.

"Mmm, baby," she said when she caught him noticing her. "What is that?"

"Don't know yet." He still wasn't listening to himself, focused instead on the cascade of memories—flowing faster now—passing before his eyes. Through the guitar he poured them all below, letting them fall to the courtyard until Gideon could envision playing out all of himself down there. Then, he would lean over the railing and the essence of him would either catch the empty shell or let it shatter against the pavement. And he didn't much care which.

Movement below caught his attention. A man had stepped out from the shadows—hairy and bedraggled face, dressed in a stained t-shirt and pants that looked even filthier in the yellow glow of the alley streetlights. He gazed upwards, not grooving to the music like club-go-ers might, but drinking it in. A tingling sensation ran through Gideon, making his cheeks flush. He stole a glance at Caron, but she didn't appear to notice anyone else but him. Her lips had parted and he could see her pulse fluttering beneath the skin at her throat. Its tempo quick-ened in time with the electric scream building in Gideon's fingers. The guitar was like a bare wire in his grip that he couldn't bear to hold onto, and yet couldn't put down.

He looked down again. The man had raised his left arm, palm to-ward the sky, almost as if offering something. Then he lifted the other hand, holding something between his fingers that glinted in the light. Gideon's heart pounded—steady, hammering blows as if it were trying to batter its way out of his chest. The alley-man touched his right hand to his left wrist and started to draw down. The skin gave way as if along a seam. Gideon's guitar screeched even louder in his ears. The alley-man's eyes opened wide—wider—wider still—until Gideon felt the heat of their gaze like a spotlight. His own arms burned, but he couldn't stop, couldn't leave the song unfinished even as the music itself was cutting him open, then spattering to the pavement in a rain of blood.

But then, somehow, it did suddenly stop. Gideon stood, waiting for reality to reboot itself and dispel the hallucination he was most cer-tainly having. But the man was still there, now slowly turning away. Gideon's whole body tingled as if his skin had suddenly grown a million tiny legs, which were now trying to crawl off his bones. For a moment he was stuck as the world congealed around him again. Then he was face-to-face with Caron. Her eyes stared hungrily and when she pressed her body against his, her warmth and her fragrance overwhelmed him. Gideon leaned forward, slipped his lips onto hers, and his body nearly exploded.

Caron brought her car to a stop at the intersection with the lights of Honest John's nightclub beckoning from the end of the next block.

"The light was yellow," Gideon said. "You totally could've made it."

"Run all the yellows you want in your own car. I ain't gonna get t-boned because of you."

"I'm late." Despite the air-conditioning blasting through the vents, Gideon's shirt clung to his skin under his arms and across the small of his back. The heat and humidity made even the air sweat; it lay heavily over the city, lulling it into an almost narcotic stupor. People on the sidewalks, the traffic around them, even the flashing messages from billboards and storefronts seemed to move in slow-motion.

"Not my fault," Caron responded, and a pins-and-needles sensation inside him surged a little stronger. He had a sudden moment of being unable to recall if he'd actually invited her to his gig tonight, or if she'd just assumed she could come. That was her style, as he'd discovered. Do whatever she wants and wait for someone to dare tell her "no."

The traffic light turned green, and Caron nudged her car through the crowd swarming in front of the club entrance. She hadn't even come to a full stop before Gideon swung the passenger door open and hit the pavement, already hurrying around to the trunk. "Pop it!" he called. Caron shifted into park and fiddled with something on the dashboard. Gideon slapped the car. "Pop it!"

"Gimme a second!" Caron hollered back. "Jesus!" A *click*, and the latch released. Gideon threw the trunk open all the way and lifted his guitar case out. His blood was already running hotter than the summer night, causing fresh stains to spread along his collar. *Or maybe*, he thought, he could feel the heat so much more than before. Back in "The Day" (as he thought of his past), an awesome high left him feeling like he was walking on the edge of a knife. Since that night on his fire escape however, he *was* the edge. Just thinking of the alley-man made his senses buzz. The city was still as dingy and stench-ridden as ever, but it couldn't touch him. He sliced through the pollution so cleanly that it didn't even bleed on him.

He slammed the lid closed a little harder than he'd intended, suddenly revealing Caron in a light purple camisole and hip-hugging leather skirt that made every curve of her body into a work of art. The glare in her eyes, however, chilled the rising interest in his pants. "Easy on the car," she warned, "or you're walking home."

"I'm late," he offered again. "Tell Curtis at the door you're with me and he'll get you in." Gideon turned away before he finished speaking and jogged down the side alley. It seemed a mile long tonight and all he wanted to do was get inside and get to playing. Touch even a little piece of how he was feeling inside.

If the bullshit of the world didn't bring him back down first.

The stage door opened just as he drew near and Booker—the drummer—stuck his head out with a mischievous grin lighting his face.

"Not a fuckin' word," Gideon said, mounting the steps two at a time. Booker stepped back and with a mocking half-bow, invited him inside. As Gideon burst through, he caught another shit-eating grin from Ray-Ray, bass-guitar. He crossed to the middle of the backstage to set his case on a folding table, all the while avoiding eye contact with Marcus. However, all six-foot-four of the man started rumbling towards him, his face a deeper black than Gideon would have imagined possible.

"I hate it when you're late," Marcus growled over Gideon's shoulder. "It drives me crazy, you know that. It fuckin' drives me crazy when you're late."

Gideon swung the guitar strap over his head giving Marcus a partially accidental shove with his elbow. "That what yo' Daddy said to yo' Mama?"

Booker and Ray-Ray each barked out a laugh. "All right fools, time to get to work," Marcus bellowed. He poked Gideon with an index finger thick as a sausage. "That's fifty you don't get for missin' load-in, and fifty more for missin' sound check."

Gideon kept his mouth closed even as the hair bristled on the back of his neck. He was in the wrong—he knew that—and had nothing to gain from a throw-down with Marcus right before a show. Yet this rational thought did nothing to soothe the pounding in his temples. The heat in his veins surged, almost to the point of bursting through his eyes and burning everything within sight in a grand inferno. He found an odd satisfaction in that thought: the stage surrounded by curtains of flame, choking smoke, Marcus melted and charred like a marshmallow dropped onto campfire coals.

Out on stage, Gideon plugged into an amplifier and snuck a peek through a gap in the curtains. A raucous crowd had jammed themselves into the club, dancing shoulder-to-shoulder to the house music. If Caron had been able to get in, he couldn't see her. *Shouldn't've made us late*, he thought.

As the DJ music faded out and the stage lights came on, a fresh wave of heat flooded over him and Gideon's collar seemed to shrink an inch on the spot. Then, the stage curtains swung open and he thrashed an opening that drew cheers. "American Woman"—one of their better covers. Marcus began scream-singing into the microphone, sending the crowd immediately into a frenzy. A big man with even bigger lungs, he barely needed any amplification. His natural speaking voice had a rumbling timbre that could be heard a hundred feet away and when he sang, the roof shook.

Gideon's fingers danced across the strings. He felt himself step back inside, waiting for something to wash up and through him as before. Nothing happened except that he fell out of time with the rest of the band. The itch wasn't there: the pinprick sensation all over his body that demanded release. He looked for it in his memory of the fire escape when there had been real music. His music. All he was playing now were notes and chords—and wrong ones at that. His heart rose into his throat as the idea now came to him that what he'd taken for clarity was actually emptiness.

He caught sideways glares from the rest of the band. The song was about to crash when at last something reached up and seized him. A tingling. A sound. A song from somewhere far away and deep inside him all at the same time. Gideon let just a little of its tone out through his hands, like opening a chink in a garden hose. Memories that didn't belong to him flew past his eyes, accompanied by sensations he'd never felt. The audience roared, and the energy pumped into Gideon's body like air into a balloon—stretching him toward bursting. The only release was blasting it back out through the Strat, which made the crowd cheer even louder and pump him even more. Off to the side, Gideon glimpsed the stage hand running the mixer wrestle with the sound balance. *Fuck you*, he thought. *Balance this.*

Marcus shot an angry glance over his shoulder that Gideon knew he was supposed to be intimidated by, but it never touched him. He was going critical—a reactor smashing atom after atom in a round of pinball. Gideon could feel it happening even as a sensation of cool had started to envelop him. Marcus kept pushing, his cheeks turning purple from the exertion. "GONNA LEAVE YA, WOMAN!" he screeched, pumping his voice as hard as he could. But his body started to shake. Gideon's power, on the other hand, surged—sweeping him out of the flow of time. Within the span of a split-second he made eye contact with each and every reveler in the club and dove into their souls. They were as open to him as if their hearts and minds had been filleted. He saw the fears of the things they'd touched, or the things which had touched them. Their petty worries and their real ones. He knew where they were bleeding and rotting even if they didn't.

"BYE—BYE!" Marcus screamed. "BYE—BYE!" And then the big man hitched as if someone had grabbed his balls and pulled them up to his chest. The clubgoers closest to the stage flinched. Their dance transformed into a retreat, their cheers becoming screams. Red mist sprayed from Marcus's mouth just as the man-mountain came crashing from the rounded peak of his bald head all the way to the floor. He hit with dead weight—three-hundred pounds striking with twice as much force. The impact shook the entire stage, rattling Booker's drums and popping sound jacks out of their ports. For a moment, the screech of feedback drowned out all other cries.

Booker and Ray-Ray rushed to Marcus's side. Only gradually did Gideon realize that he was still playing. He willed his hands to stop moving—even tried to force them up into the air—but they wouldn't obey. He literally had to tear them from the guitar and as soon as he did, the sensation of his own body came flooding back to him. Every muscle burned as if he'd been twisted like a rubber band on a toy propeller and then suddenly released.

The crowd, which had fled Marcus's seizure, now seeped forward to get a better view. Blood covered the stage and dance floor like a gruesome Pollock painting. Gideon could not lift his stare from the big man's body until the ambulance crew was climbing onto the stage. It took both EMTs and all three band members to lift Marcus onto the stretcher. The medics slapped a respirator over his face, but from the speed with which the color had already drained from his flesh, even Gideon could tell that the man was gone.

The band followed the stretcher out the front of the club and helped again to load it into the ambulance. The instant the rear doors closed, it sped off in a storm of lights and sirens. Gideon's shock began to peel away as the crowd on the sidewalk dispersed. Part of him felt sad. Only a part. The rest rejoiced. He had been playing Music—as in Music the Primal Force, not just another assemblage of notes and chords. It had come so naturally, like the song last week on the fire escape.

It was easy, he thought. *Easy as breathing.*

He felt dizzy. His vision seemed to spin in full circles until it fixed on a parade of rags on the sidewalk across the street. The homeless in his neighborhood usually gathered in groups of three or four at the most, but here stood fifteen to twenty. Not a single face was unmangled in one way or another. Scarred cheeks where the shaving razor had sliced too long and too deep. Black and red burns. Rusted nails, needles and safety pins hanging from folds of the flesh. They held themselves so perfectly still that Gideon came close to doubting their reality, except that he felt their presence like the heat from a bed of coals waiting to be breathed into flame again.

Gideon recognized the man in the center. Bloodstains still covered the alley-man's t-shirt and his right arm was bandaged from wrist to shoulder with soiled strips of fabric. *He's brought others*, Gideon thought. Not just fans, though. Inspirations. Causes for song.

In the alley-man's opposite hand, he held out the broken bottom of a glass beer bottle, its jagged rim resting points-down on the flesh of his palm. With a smile of pure serenity, he clenched his hand into a fist. Blood leaked freely through his fingers—heavy drops falling and spreading out in a pool of red. Gideon heard—or rather, felt—his own body start to vibrate. Music swelled inside him, tracing the songs in his bones to screams of birth and death, joy and pain. Ten thousand years' and billions of lives' worth roared through him, pounding in his ears and in his heart.

Then, seemingly by force of will, the alley-man's wound stopped flowing and with it, the singing chord in Gideon's bones faded like an old radio signal slipping over the horizon. The alley-man turned away first, and then as one, the rest of the crowd dissipated into the night. Gideon watched until the last of them had gone. On the street, surrounded by the traffic and the city-dwellers going to and fro on their own journeys, loneliness settled over his heart like a shroud.

He spun around and headed back inside the club to get his guitar.

It took a good three hours to walk home, crisscrossing the city streets as if in a dream, unable to remember the events of the night as fact instead of fantasy. He passed a handful of people along his way—and usually at a distance—but even so, they all seemed to have a touch of Marcus in them. Sometimes it was the way the eyes narrowed into a stare, or the curl of the lips. Gideon shrugged off the blame these faces wanted to lay on him. It wasn't his fault, he hadn't done anything. He was just playing his…

Music.

It was all around him—he couldn't believe he'd never heard it before. The hum of the streetlights thundered in his ears. The reverberations of cars rattling by. And more. He heard people he didn't even see. The ones inside the cars, behind drawn windows, in the shadows between buildings that he walked by. *Was this how Jimmy Page walked through the world?* he wondered. *Or Stevie Ray Vaughn? Or Hendrix?* Gideon had tasted something, and it aroused a hunger he never knew he had, the way the brush of a kiss electrifies the whole skin. He hadn't even remembered leaving Caron back at Honest John's until he was halfway back to his apartment. Even then, she existed as an afterthought, just like the other revelers. They listened to his music, but brought little in return. No real fuel for the fire.

Fire.

Even after climbing the stairs to his apartment and setting the guitar on the couch, he kept walking. He paced the length of the apartment from kitchen to front bay window, pausing each time to glance at the bar and package store sitting side by side across the street. He imagined them burning, the same way he had envisioned the stage at the club burning, and the idea possessed him with such reality that he could actually hear the crackle of the flames and feel the smoke tickle the inside of his nose and throat.

Somehow, although he couldn't remember doing it, the guitar case sat open. Vibrations ran from Gideon's fingertips all the way up to his shoulders every time he passed by. He knew the Shakes—nicotine shakes, heroin shakes, detox shakes—but nothing like this. The guitar was making promises as clearly as if the words had actually been spoken.

At last he took it up, not caring that the only sounds coming forth were feeble *whumps*. The Music was within him—and beyond him at the same time. Back and forth through the apartment he walked until the sky lightened. The phone rang a couple of times. He ignored it. A stabbing pain made its home in one knee. Blisters formed on the pads of his fingers, broke open and drained to the floor, but the pain couldn't reach him. Hunger could not reach him, nor thirst. The Music became his whole world, everything he knew.

By the time the sun went down again, Gideon had found his melody. It looped over itself so that one chord had barely faded before the next sounded. And then another, and another, all the way around to the first one again—the sound of an entire symphony coming from one instrument.

As night asserted itself, Gideon walked out onto the fire escape. The darkness rolled away from him the way that flame beats back the shadows and sets them to dancing. Across the courtyard, his audience had already gathered. No speakers, no amps, and yet from the alleys and ruins and lost places of the city they had heard him. Heard, and come. He spied one woman holding a long, jagged shard of glass. She pressed her palms together, rubbing them tightly when he turned to play for her. Tears running down greasy cheeks met the upturned ends of her smiling lips. Gideon felt as if his own flesh were tearing open, yet didn't back away from the sensation or hold it for himself. He poured it all into his instrument, shredding new chords he'd never played before. Whole new sounds roared through him—a language of piercings, rippings, burnings, bleedings from a hundred other souls within reach of his concert. He found music for them all.

Any sense of time melted away. He felt like he'd been playing for forever plus a day when Caron's sedan pulled into the lot. His audience made themselves into ghosts, disappearing into corners as if they'd never been there at all. Gideon's fingers never left his strings. Caron looked up at him the moment she stepped out of the car and hollered something he couldn't hear. She was one of the Others—always had been, but now Gideon could tell the difference. The Others were all fools or liars, either ignorant of what true Music sounded like, or else in denial. They were deaf and mute, and playing for them was meaningless because they could not hear the discord that was part of the melody, or the cacophony inside the melody. They were half-people, living half-lives. The Music was not for them.

She needed to leave, and leave now. But instead, Caron started coming up the fire escape, calling to him with her silent voice. *Them*, he wanted to tell her. *Them!* Gideon sensed a ripple pass through the invisible crowd around her. Dark figures stepped forward, like the fingers of a lengthening shadow. *Be my Music*, he pleaded silently. Caron climbed the steps to his landing. He watched her mouth shape the sounds of his name. A part of him—distant and faint—remembered how she had tasted, but even in that memory he found nothing to play. She had nothing for him. She was a foreign presence—an invader.

Now Caron reached his landing, shouting and waving her arms and not once noticing the throng that had followed her up the stairs. Gideon tried to speak, but his voice would not come forth any louder than a whisper. She stomped towards him and all he could do was shake his head as she clapped one hand across the guitar's neck and wrenched it from him. For the first time in nearly twenty-four hours, Gideon stopped playing. Strand by strand, the web holding his audience to him stretched, then tore. The muscles in his legs gave out and he collapsed.

Caron dropped the guitar and leaned over him. "Are you fucked up?" she hollered. "Is that what this is all about? I don't take this kind of shit from no—"

The hand dropping on her shoulder cut her off in mid-rant. She whirled around so that Gideon couldn't see her reaction to the burnt, scarred faces encircling her. She screamed—an honest sound—as a dozen bloodied, grimy hands pulled her off her feet and down the fire escape. Gideon trembled as broken bottles, pipes, and even fingernails and teeth, laid siege to her skin. Being without Music, they crafted some for her out of the cracking of her jaw and the wet *rip* of her limbs, twisting until the flesh and the muscles tore and gave way. A dagger of glass slashed across her face, slicing one eye open like a grape. Her blood pattered in a syncopated rhythm that somehow Gideon could hear high above her cries which sang out across the courtyard.

Heavy smoke rolled over a nearby rooftop, glowing red-orange light from the inferno beneath it. Gideon could smell it, searing the inside of his chest, but that wasn't the reason he felt his gut start to spoil and his mouth fill with the taste of rotten meat. Distant shouts and sirens filled the air, but all he could hear was Caron's requiem. Her death, so brutal and so near (*so innocent!*), curdled the Music inside him.

Not Music, he realized. Something that was breaking apart the world around him instead of bringing it together. He didn't have a word to describe what it was that he'd taken into himself. A hunger outside of himself, an appetite for suffering. And the alley-people had it now, as they frolicked to a tune only they could hear. The Music had passed through Gideon and left behind a fever to consume him like paper in flame.

He lunged for his guitar, but only succeeded in nudging it farther away. Cramped muscles struggled to obey, and the best he could manage was an inching crawl. The heat was dissolving him from the inside, and the pressure in his head felt like a hammer beating at him from behind his own eyes. If he could play it out, like before, send the song into the night…

The Strat was so close…

It started in his hands—they who had dutifully endured the soreness and the calluses of thousands of hours of play. They exploded into flame. Gideon screamed, and down in the courtyard below his audience roared. He felt one last surge roll through him like the tide, and then his fever lit him like a torch. His body exploded, engulfing the upper third of the building façade. The wood and brick seemed to scream while the fire licked the sky.

Below, the alley-people danced in the choking smoke. For those with the sensitivity to hear, the cacophony of the city harmonized. The Music called out in a single tone that echoed through the canyons of brick, stone and steel. Like the ripples from a stone cast into still waters, it spread further and further in order to gather its children.

Listen…

Listen…

Straw Man

The thing crossed the road right in front of him.

Peter had not fallen asleep—not in the traditional sense, anyway. His eyes were on the road and foot on the gas pedal, but by the time he'd come off the interstate and the state route, his hands had taken control of the wheel. They remembered the twists and turns of the county roads as if they were still part of his daily routine, leaving his mind free to flip through the pages of its own scrapbook. He remembered coming down this road for the first time, on the near side of eight years old in the back of a sheriff's car with a suitcase of donated clothes bouncing on the seat beside him. He remembered the barn behind Aunt Dodie and Uncle David's house and the hay loft where he used to take his girlfriends…

He remembered how warm Sharon had felt beneath him, and yet how cold her eyes. Silence blanketed them—only her breath escaping in tiny gasps each time he pushed into her made even the slightest suggestion of a sound…

The ache in his knuckles pulled him out of his reverie. He was strangling the steering wheel as if fighting to keep from turning around. He wouldn't know how to explain that to Aunt Dodie. She was all alone on the farm now that Uncle David was dead.

…thoughtless little boy…

127

Some part of his mind still on active duty spotted the shape in the road—two legs, upright. Peter slammed on the brakes but the gravel road gave his worn tires very little to grab onto. The car started to fishtail, then swung around a hundred degrees before stopping on the opposite shoulder. At first, he just sat there, unable to move while the adrenaline rush still had his brain set on a spin cycle. After a minute or so, he turned to look for the shape in the road. A face in the windshield glass caught his attention instead, grabbing him and holding him in place. Dark, hollow eyes worked their way up and down his body leaving a prickling sensation, like a sunburn, in its wake.

The straw man.

Of all things, he caught himself thinking of the scarecrow that used to stand in Aunt Dodie's vegetable garden. The wizened gourd it used for a head peered through the window of the old den converted to his bedroom. Although no one had ever painted or carved a face on it, the wrinkles and pits and moonlight shadows created a wide variety of expressions. Peter knew them all because the one constant was the stare—knowing his secrets as surely as if they'd been tattooed across his flesh. Closed curtains or not, its gaze never wavered from the window, and that's how he knew what the straw man saw.

It saw everything.

The flash of recollection lasted only an instant before the face in the windshield reshaped itself into his own reflection. *Too tired*, he thought, stepping out of the car. The road was empty except for whatever his imagination had conjured from the twilight spaces between his awake and dreaming minds. His eyes took in the surrounding fields full of bushy soybean plants a couple feet high, glowing with a bluish tint under the low moon.

The field on his left sloped gently to a hillock with a copse of oak trees on the crest and even though it was out of sight, he pictured clearly the way the land slipped down the other side, creating a tidy eighty acre pocket. The farmhouse could be found near the open end, the old barn standing hard by.

He could see it all without seeing it. He was home.

When Peter awoke in his old bed, his immediate impression was that the last ten years had been an elaborate dream. He expected to see his fleet of model warships on top of the dresser and old Neil O'Donnell posters on the wall. The decorations were all gone, but otherwise the room looked just as it had the day he'd left for college. That surprised him. He knew other people called it "blessed" that family had taken him in after his parents died, but he was sure there had been some celebration when the decade-long houseguest finally took his leave.

He swung off the blankets and grabbed a sweatshirt and a pair of jeans from his suitcase. A manila envelope came out with the clothes, falling to the floor. A week after Uncle David's funeral, his aunt's neighbor—Bill Yoder—had called to ask about the family's intentions for the farm. *Burn it*, was Peter's instinctive response, but he listened to a carefully polite sales pitch and even before hanging up, had decided to call a lawyer friend about drawing up a purchase agreement for Aunt Dodie to sign.

But would she? She'd probably resist at first, and he could understand that. So much happening so quickly. But Yoder's offer would set her up at the Pine Acres apartments—away from the farm. Walking through the door last night, Peter could tell the house was just as full of memories now as when he'd left. They spilled into the hallways, stacked themselves in every corner and even if Aunt Dodie's remembrances were nothing like his (*Please God*, he prayed), they would never die so long as any one of them remained.

And if some of the sale money came to him, he admitted to thinking, he could get a new situation for himself, too. Somehow Youngstown had become very small. He caught himself expecting to see Sharon every time he turned a street corner or walked down the aisle in a store.

She came to his apartment. She smelled so clean, so good...

Peter wandered out onto the front porch. The morning sun peeking over the horizon cast a very different image of the farm he had seen last night. The plants looked full—like they were supposed to—but dull in color, sagging back to the earth instead of stretching for the sky. The sight made him frown as he settled into Uncle David's aluminum porch chair and tried to remember if the purchase agreement included anything about Ag Commission inspections.

Tipping back in his seat, he let his hand casually fall down and to the right until his fingers brushed against a glass bottle tucked into a hidey-hole in the brick of the porch. Uncle David's secret Canadian V.O., mostly empty by the feel of it. A fifteen-year predecessor to this bottle had taught Peter a new way to get through the night when the gaze of the straw man wouldn't stop flooding through his bedroom window, and if Uncle David had ever wondered why his liquor evaporated so quickly... well, there hadn't been much he could do about it. Chalk it up to one more secret the two of them shared.

Peter brought his empty hand back to his lap. Had Uncle David indulged himself before heading out to the field? The accident was just one of those things, as Aunt Dodie told it. Brakes on the tractor locked up coming down the slope. It flipped and crushed Uncle David, squeezing the air from his lungs and soaking the earth with his blood. Aunt Dodie had been out shopping—he'd lain there most of the afternoon and into the evening before one of the Yoder boys noticed the overturned tractor and came rushing over.

Hearing about it over the phone was as surreal as anything Peter could imagine. Another voice—another person, it seemed—from inside said he had an important assignment for the newspaper the same week as the funeral. He didn't remember exactly what happened next; one moment he was rushing from room to room to close all the curtains, and then the bottle of Jameson's appeared in his hand. After two drinks, the stare of the scarecrow from his mind's eye started to burn a little less fiercely. Sharon might have come by later to see why he'd missed work. Somehow they ended up together on his couch...

...*thoughtless little boy*...

The voice echoed so loudly that Peter wasn't sure if he'd heard it only in his head or if someone had actually bellowed the words. Quickly he looked out across the field and caught an eyeful of sunlight stabbing all the way to the back of his head. In the center of the glare he saw a silhouetted figure, arms stretched out to either side like Christ on the cross. No face was visible, yet Peter knew with the kind of certainty reserved for nightmares that the shape was looking right at him.

Close your eyes and it'll go away, he told himself—even though he knew damn well that wasn't true. You could squeeze your lids closed and hold them until it hurt, but it never once had made his skin stop tingling, nor stopped the mattress springs from squeaking, nor kept the straw man from watching.

Gradually the burst of red and orange cleared, but the vision of the scarecrow remained—not off in the distance, but standing its post in the vegetable garden next to the house. Peter blinked until he convinced himself he was staring at something that was actually there. The straw man's clothes hung loosely off its frame, enough so that the morning breeze caught them like a sail and turned the figure a quarter-turn away.

Peter watched it closely for any possible nod of the head, or roll of the shoulder, or flex of the hips. Any signal that the thing was turning back again.

Turning back to look at him.

The screen door behind him squeaked open, making him jump in his seat. "Ooh, I thought I heard you up and about," Aunt Dodie cooed. Forty-eight years of teaching first grade had ingrained the habit of speaking in a singsong voice like a bargain-rate Glinda the Good. Peter stood and navigated around the two mugs of coffee she was carrying to give her a quick hug.

"Here." She handed him one. "You still like it no sugar, just a splash of milk?"

He nodded as a bitter tang reached his nose. *Ugh*, he thought. "How old is this?"

"Three days. That's farmer's coffee, as your uncle would say." Aunt Dodie shuffled past him, swaying slightly like a church bell. At the foot of the porch steps, she stopped and pointed at a metal pail full of greens. "Bring that and you can help me with the rabbits."

Peter caught himself smiling. "You still keep rabbits?"

"A few. Ain't good for much. Can't take 'em to fair no more."

Aunt Dodie set off for the barn. Peter hustled down the porch steps after her, grabbing the pail in stride. If there was one chore from his youth he genuinely liked, it had been tending the rabbits—usually fed leftovers and undesirables from Aunt Dodie's garden. When he glanced at the pail's contents now, however, he almost stopped short. None of it looked fit for consumption. Like the soybeans, the broccoli and spinach looked dull and flaccid—nearly more grey in color than green.

"I don't know if I told you," he said, catching up to his aunt, "but Bill Yoder called a couple weeks ago. He really went on about how nice Uncle David's service was."

"Most everybody was there."

Peter tried to let the barb go by, but caught himself making a smile out of a grimace anyway. "He had something else to talk about. Something for you and I both to talk about, really."

Aunt Dodie made no response, not even a sign that she'd heard him, although he did catch her peeking at him over her shoulder as they reached the barn. She was all smiles, however, by the time she started wrestling with the door, giving it two or three good shakes before sliding it open. Peter followed her one step inside before a stench that could only have come from every old dead thing he had ever come across nearly dropped him in the doorway: decomposing deer in roadside ditches, plus cat, skunk, and raccoon carcasses shredded by some other animal—throats torn open and bled dry, ropes of entrails spilled out through belly wounds, their eyes and mouths stretched open in a final snarl against death. As a concoction, it curdled the spit in his mouth.

"What the hell happened in here?" he said.

"Oh, it ain't that bad," Aunt Dodie answered. "C'mon if you're comin'."

Peter clamped down on his somersaulting stomach and carried the pail to the rabbit hutches standing against the right-hand wall. They used to keep about two dozen animals in the barn, and he once had a bulletin board full of 4-H ribbons as a testament to the quality of his care. Here now were ten raggedy creatures of normal size and weight but their eyes were vacant, their coats somehow dingy without being dirty.

Peter set the pail down between him and his aunt and swung open the door to the first hutch. The rabbit sat in the far corner, not twitching so much as a whisker. "Aunt Dodie?" he asked.

"Hm?"

"Did you hear what I said?"

"The Yoders," she muttered, dropping a handful of limp spinach in front of twin lop-ears. "They have enough land. They don't need any more from us."

Peter's heart skipped. "What do you mean?"

"Mr. Yoder called yesterday afternoon wanting to know if you'd arrived yet and what time would be good to come by and sign the papers." Her voice started to crack and Peter swore he could see her start to wear her age. The blush in her cheeks turned sallow and the kindly crinkles around her eyes and mouth became deep gouges in her skin. "I told him not to bother."

The surprise made Peter suck in a deeper breath than he'd intended and a fresh gulp of the barn-stench nearly made him gag. "Why did you do that?"

"Why do you think?"

Four different thoughts crashed into each other in Peter's head and he struggled to decide which one to give voice to. "I'm sorry," he stammered, "I thought this was a way for you to get a nest egg for retirement."

"Retirement's for other folk," Aunt Dodie said.

"You can't do all this work by yourself."

"I'm not by myself. You're here."

"For the weekend. Not for good."

Aunt Dodie looked into his eyes and smiled as if trying to beam it into him. "But this farm is going to be yours someday."

"Mine?" A vision of the blighted crops filled his head. "What am I supposed to do with it?"

"David taught you everything he knew. Like his father did for him."

Peter's jaw tightened. "He's not my father."

"Mind your manners." Aunt Dodie's lips pursed and thinned. "I never said he was. But you were raised here. This family takes care of this land. It's not for anyone else to do."

"Uncle David's family, maybe. Not ours."

"It's ours now. We've eaten its food, put our own hard work and sacrifice into it."

Peter sighed. "Look at the fields. Look at your own garden. Bill Yoder obviously thinks he can still do something with the soil—let him have it."

He started to step back, but Aunt Dodie caught him by the wrist. He winced, half from surprise and half from her sudden vise-like grip. "I know David was…hard on you," she said in a hushed voice, "but it was hard for him, too. He had to work twice as hard as everyone else to have the same things. The house. His family. I don't know why—that's just how it was."

A lump rose in Peter's throat. *From guilt?* he wondered. "I'm not a farmer."

"You're a good boy. I know you'll do the right thing." Aunt Dodie released his arm, but her stare held him close. "And it isn't as if you'll be alone."

A breeze wafted into the barn, cleansing the air at least for a moment. Peter faced the open doorway to catch as much of it as he could and noticed that the same wind must've caught the straw man's clothes again and turned it now toward the barn.

"I see you put a new scarecrow in the garden," he said.

Aunt Dodie upended the pail over the last cage. "He's always been there," she replied.

Deep into the night, Peter closed his eyes and leaned against the vinyl back of the kitchen chair. *Nope*, he decided. Not even a little drowsy. The hands of the rooster clock over the sink had wound just past two a.m.—over an hour since he'd given up the chase for sleep and left his bedroom in search of a drink (of water, he admonished himself) to relieve the layer of cotton coating the inside of his mouth. But the water from the faucet had a mineral smell that wrinkled his nose, so he just sat at the kitchen table marveling at the true darkness of the country night. He'd almost forgotten how deep and silent it could be—enough so to feel the thrumming of some kind of presence. *The power of the land?* he wondered. *Mother Nature?* A machine with a thousand gears, any one of which out of alignment was the difference between a harvest and a patch of dirt.

Or something else. The crops had come up this year—obviously— but not how they should. Even he knew it wasn't a matter of neglect or disease. The farm was just…wrong. Peter shook his head. *This is what Aunt Dodie wants me to take over?* Farming wasn't his bloodline, not his heritage. He liked city living—stores open after 8 p.m., movie theatres with current releases, pizza delivery.

He'd answered the knock at his door with a spoiled taste in his mouth and a greasy sensation all over his skin. Sharon stood in the doorway, smelling as clean as the rain. Sometimes that fragrance would waft over the divider between their cubicles at work and make it hard for him to concentrate. So pure. So good. A touch from her could make him feel the way he wanted to feel…

He blinked furiously to clear the memories away and found himself staring out the kitchen window at the old barn on the other side of the dirt and gravel driveway. Not exactly the tree house he'd fantasized about, but it offered lots more places to play in if one didn't mind getting really, truly filthy. Following an afternoon in there, Uncle David would greet him with three separate and distinct whippings: one for skipping chores, one for not coming immediately when called, and one for looking and smelling so foul. The finale of the last beating always took place in the upstairs bathroom, where Uncle David made him strip and climb into the claw-foot tub. Little Peter would sit on the chipped and cracked bottom with his knees tucked under his chin, waiting for the first burst of cold water to hit.

"You're a thoughtless little boy," Uncle David said, holding Peter by one wrist while he scrubbed. The soap made his rough hands smooth and slippery as they roamed down Peter's chest, across his backside and between his legs. Innocent contact—almost accidental—but then came banishment to his bedroom and the wait until the farm fell dark. The bedroom door would creak open and the springs squeak at the foot of his mattress. Peter learned to turn his head away and stare out the window.

To meet the gaze of the straw man.

Outside the kitchen, the wind picked up, carrying a sound like someone walking through a pile of dry leaves. *Forget,* his inside-voice told him as a dull ache began to nest in his forehead. He leaned forward to stand, to walk to the porch and the whiskey, when he suddenly froze instead. The wind had died away but the soft and steady crunching sound continued. Peter pressed himself back against the chair as far as he could, wishing he could pull the shadows around him like a cloak. The footsteps traveled the length of the house, past the kitchen and around to his bedroom. A window slid open, letting in a chill that ebbed and flowed like a cycle of breath.

Peter's chest tightened, waiting for the gaze of the straw man to find him even through the walls of the house. Another set of footsteps approached—from inside the house this time, coming down the stairs. Aunt Dodie turned the corner, fully-dressed in the yellow polo shirt and full-length denim skirt she wore around the farm like a uniform. She hurried past the kitchen without a sideways glance, down the hall and into Peter's bedroom.

Silence. Then Aunt Dodie's hushed whispers floated through the stillness: "I don't know…out drinking…you remember what he was like…"

The window in his bedroom slid closed again, and the panic freezing Peter in the chair relaxed its hold just enough for him to sneak into the shadows of the kitchen. He pressed himself against the counter on the far side of the refrigerator as Aunt Dodie shuffled by, pausing only long enough to grab her barn coat from the coat rack before heading out the back door.

Long minutes passed while Peter held himself still as stone. When he felt safe to move again, he crept back by the table to look out the window. The light inside the barn framed its large doors in a yellow glow. A commanding blend of dread and curiosity summoned him and before he truly realized what he was doing, he had walked outside and crossed halfway to the barn. Within several steps of the doors, he took back enough control to circle around to the side. Stone steps led down to a splintering wooden doorway. The pungent, sweet odor of old earth swept into his nose as he slipped inside. Shafts of light fell through the floorboards, revealing the outlines of wooden crates, newspaper bundles, and lawn equipment. Shelves of mason jars and cobwebbed bottles lined the walls.

Peter stopped to listen to shambling footsteps from above and nervous chirping from the rabbits. One of the cage doors opened. A moment later he heard Aunt Dodie grunt with exertion, then a cracking noise followed instantly by a hatchet blade biting into wood. A metal pail was set down, the handle banging against its side. Peter's stomach turned a somersault as something wet and heavy made a glop hitting the bottom of the pail. From above, he could sense a presence—like feeling the heat off a fire before seeing the actual flames. Peter headed for the stairs leading to the main floor, passing a rack of rusted tools. He paused for a moment before taking an ice chipper from its hook on the wall.

Overhead, Aunt Dodie hummed "Shall We Gather at the River." Even so, every squeak and groan of the steps exploded in his ears. About halfway up, Peter stopped to peek through the railing. The sour, rotten stench again assaulted his senses and now he could see the source. A scarecrow—not the one from the garden, but the one that had stared at him from the horizon this morning—reclined in an Adirondack deck chair as if it were sunning itself, a rabbit carcass crumpled at its feet. The clothes it wore were Uncle David's—an old flannel shirt and jean coveralls worn threadbare in the knees—but instead of being made of sticks and straw, this creature had leathery skin, stinking of rot and stretched tautly to the point where it split open along sharp edges of bone. It had no eyes—only a frigid darkness reaching out from within its husk of a skull.

Aunt Dodie stood nearby with the pail in one hand, ladling the contents into the straw man's mouth with a large spoon. As Peter stared, he

felt a blacksmith set up shop behind his temples, sending bright pounding pain through his head. It knocked him out of any sense of time or
place so that when he stopped wincing and opened his eyes, he was
suddenly staring into Sharon's face. The fragrance of her skin—chamo-
mile and almond—made his blood run hot while she felt so, so cool.
He laid her back and tugged off her jeans and underwear. She may have
moaned in protest once but by then he was on top of her, laying his
forearm across her collarbone. *Don't move*, he ordered. Her eyes turned
cold, then blank, and he watched the sparkle in them retreat in a way
her body could not. It was like staring into his own memory.

...dirty boy...

Like flipping a channel, his world suddenly snapped back to the
barn. Aunt Dodie and the scarecrow had both turned to look at him.
Peter tightened his grip around the ice chipper's handle, ignoring the
wood slivers stabbing into his flesh as he climbed the rest of the stairs.
At the top, he shot a glance at his aunt and she blushed.

"You see?" she said. "The land gave your father back to us. It knows
how much we need him."

The back of Peter's neck grew hot. "He's not my father."

"He raised you!" Aunt Dodie's cheeks flushed from pink to an angry
rose color. "Like his father raised him. He made you who you are!"

The smell of Uncle David's pipe tobacco sliced through the barn-
stench to fill Peter's mouth and nose. He struggled to make his arms
obey—to heft the chipper like a spear—even as a ghostly, yet familiar, crushing grip tightened around his wrist. He rushed the creature,
guiding the chipper blade straight for the scarecrow's chest. It stopped
several inches short of its mark as shriveled hands wrapped around
the wooden shaft, holding the blade at bay. Peter pushed harder. The
scarecrow's mouth worked open and closed in silent rage, billowing a
heavy, sour must into the air.

Suddenly, Peter switched from pushing to pulling and wrenched the
chipper free. He flew backwards, landing on his ass. Through the stars
dancing before his eyes, Peter saw the creature start to rise from the
deck chair.

"Stop!"

He heard Aunt Dodie's scream, but her cry barely penetrated the pounding in his head. Peter scrambled to his feet, choked up on the wooden handle and swung for the seats. The scarecrow lifted its arm in defense, but too slowly. The blade smacked the side of its head, making a crunching sound like splintering wood. Peter recovered his balance, then swung again. The straw man staggered and dropped to one knee. Its head lolled to one side, hanging below its shoulder.

…ungrateful boy…

Triumph flooded Peter's veins. He raised the chipper over his head but just as he was about to bring it crashing down, a hot pain bloomed in his lower back. Something bit deeply into flesh, muscle, and bone, then tore its way out again. The chipper fell from his hands as his legs buckled. The floor came up fast and smacked him in the teeth. Blood filled his mouth.

He turned his head. Aunt Dodie dropped the hatchet, dripping with his blood, and quickly looked away. Peter tried to stand, but his legs would only spasm in response. The straw man closed its fingers around Peter's ankles, dragging him and his open wound across the floor. The pain nearly blinded him—he clutched wildly for a handhold, scraping his fingers and palms raw against the rough hewn floor.

A few feet outside the barn, the creature flipped Peter onto his back. It bent over him, blazing with a blue and silver fire from the full moon as it pushed down on his chest. Its arms looked like kindling Peter could snap over his knee, but felt solid as iron. He struggled to crawl out from under the creature's grasp but could no longer feel his legs. A frost was spreading through his blood, leaving him so empty that he wished to feel the agony again—wished to feel anything that could anchor him before he floated away entirely.

The earth began to melt underneath him. In a panic, Peter realized he was sinking into the soil. He beat at the scarecrow's arms, but couldn't make them budge as the ground sucked on him like quicksand. *Wake up!* Peter screamed, or thought he did. But he knew that the arms pushing on his chest were real, and the power pulling him into the earth was real, and the taste of dirt in his mouth as he submerged was absolutely, unquestionably real.

The next that he knew, his body was already in motion—head and shoulders breaking through the topsoil. The chill of the night air felt like a hundred needles sticking into his face. His body weighed a ton; he had to strain just to lift his arms and brush the clumps of dirt out of his eyes.

An hour passed before Peter pulled himself out all the way. For a moment, he simply wavered on stiff yet unsteady legs. Nearby lay the old scarecrow, head still cocked at the bad angle, covered with a layer of frost.

Lamplight beckoned from the farmhouse and he shuffled towards it. Once inside, Peter headed directly to the living room. Aunt Dodie was sitting in her recliner, wrinkled feet propped up on the footrest. She smiled when she saw him.

"Such a good boy."

He opened his mouth to speak. No words came out—just rich, dark earth falling to the carpet.

Back of the Closet

Franklin knelt in the upstairs hallway, working to keep the box seams tight while he taped them together and trying very hard not to let the musty smell drive him crazy. He'd finished emptying the hall closet—that was the important thing—and he'd finally packed up all the crap that ought to have been thrown away years ago. Winter coats that had been worn only a few times before being replaced by something warmer or more fashionable were going to Goodwill. Old videotapes and DVDs were bound for the town library (if they would have them) or the "free table" (if they would not). Other items could simply be tossed in the trash—board games with missing pieces, the vacuum cleaner that didn't have good suction any more, the extra package of filters for the humidifier that he and Janice didn't own any more. Things you hold onto because maybe there might be a someday when you need them.

But, Franklin realized, in the end it was all about boxes. Brown boxes in every room stickered, taped, and labeled. Some for storage, some for moving, and some for holding stuff you didn't know what to do with. Boxes went into other boxes, stacked on top of more boxes. And there were even the boxes—like the ones laid out under his knees—too small or too old to be of use, yet too large to tuck in with the fiber recycling. The old ones smelled like wet earth. In fact, at some point—Franklin didn't know when—they all started stinking, even the brand new ones he had to buy (*Dear God*, he thought, standing in the checkout line, *Now I'm actually buying boxes*). There wasn't a room in the house he could go to escape that smell. It hung in the air like a fog.

Tighter, he reminded himself, inching the seams even closer together. No slipping or sliding allowed. That's how things fall out. That's how things get lost.

He stood, ignoring the complaining muscles in his lower back that had knotted themselves while he was bent over. They wouldn't let him straighten all the way—not at first, anyhow. But Franklin pushed through, and thin tendrils of pain snaked up his spine and around his love-handles. If Janice could see him wince, she probably would have smiled—partly to know he was in pain and partly to know that he was still capable of feeling anything at all.

He tipped the cardboard bundle against the wall and stared down the hall. Behind him, the main bathroom was empty, as was the master bedroom. The first room in front of him to the right had all the storage for the whole second floor, set aside in one place for the movers. Likewise, all of the downstairs possessions had been packed in the living room. Nothing in any of the rooms except furniture and fixtures. Everything that was going to go was ready to go.

Except…

The second smaller bedroom stood in front of Franklin, just to the right of the top of the stairs. The painted pine door gave the impression of steel somehow, keeping the room's contents sealed within (*or*, he wondered, *keeping me out?*). He had not been in his son's room for eight months. Janice, on the other hand, had hardly stepped outside of it except to eat (presumably) and then, finally, to leave the house for good. She told Franklin she was going because it was bad enough to lose Alex, but he was the one who really made her feel alone. He should've said that she was wrong, but he couldn't. He'd never been one to add more than his signature to the pre-printed sentiment in greeting cards. And what could he say anyhow? Even a year after the disappearance, the emptiness of the house crushed him, and how could he give words to such absolute nothingness?

When he finally found his voice, it was to call a realtor. The sales agent sighed and explained that while, of course, they understood the situation, they hoped that Franklin would be patient, considering the market and all. He didn't feel patient, but he did feel worn to a ghost of himself, and that would pass for patience to others. To Janice, the very idea was utterly unforgivable, and so he alone packed the house, room by room. Almost finished now.

The last room.

Alex's.

Franklin forced himself to push open the door and step inside. It had been so long that he could almost believe it was just any child's bedroom: a pleasant sage green on the walls with matching accents on the two area rugs which very nearly covered the hardwood floor between them. For all the time his wife had spent in here, she'd apparently left everything untouched. A few books for bedtime reading were still stacked on the nightstand, a couple more peeked out from underneath the head of the bed. Near the closet door lay a crumpled pile of clothes that never made it to the hamper. Even the wooden trains and plastic race cars were parked close by the toy chest instead of being put away.

The half-finished state of the room seemed to scream, *I'm not finished, Daddy…I'll come back for it later, Daddy…* Why hadn't he asked Alex to do that? Don't just dismiss the boy with a wave of the hand, but give him something specific to do. Alex wanted to go to the park with his sparkly bouncy-ball that he liked to kick down the long hallway between the front door and the kitchen—the exact same hallway which ran on the other side of the ground floor study where Franklin was trying to finish a design proposal. The project had made perfect sense the week before, but then one detail after another started going awry. He had one day to pull it all back together, but after six straight hours his own renderings started blurring together until he couldn't tell which cross-section of the building was which, and the budget numbers didn't add up, and did he really tell Alex, "Stop bouncing that goddamn ball!"? The hollow, plastic *thump-thump-thump* of the ball hitting the floor was like spraying gasoline on the fire in his head. He should have sent the boy upstairs to pick up his room. Then they could've gone to the park together afterwards. But he might've told his son just to go away. In his soul, he had to admit, that was what he wanted at the time.

And now he wanted…he wasn't sure. The hole in his heart had swallowed all of his insides. When he could still wish for things, he wished he could've been there when Alex had been taken. Even if he couldn't stop it, he'd at least have a scar. Or have been killed. Sometimes he fantasized about it—a shape as dark as night in the midst of the afternoon sun. It didn't walk through the world as much as seep like a stain through cloth. In the movie in his head, Franklin stands between the darkness and his son as the creature's arms snake toward him like tentacles. Stony knobs on its fingers batter him to his knees while the tips slice through his flesh on the backswing. The talons are so thin and sharp that Franklin doesn't even feel it at first when his skin flays open. Only as he looks down to see the ruby splashes on his clothes—and the way the Stranger's dark eyes flash with delight—does he realize the struggle is already over. He will now die, and die easily.

But at least my son gets away!

It was a comforting fantasy, even when it woke Franklin in the dead of night. Battling monsters was an honorable way to lose a child. But Alex had just been lost, like a favorite pen that you lay down someplace and can't remember where, or picked up like a newspaper left behind at the lunch counter.

Before he'd quite decided that he was going to, Franklin started picking up the clothes by the closet. His brain was lagging a minute behind his body, which was actually working out quite well. He didn't remember until after he'd put the books on their shelves about his promise that they'd start reading Lemony Snicket together now that Alex was ready for chapter books. He'd already put the sweatshirt in the drawer before connecting the brownish stain on the sleeve with Alex's attempt to play backyard football with the three fifth graders who lived up the street.

He pulled open the bi-fold doors to his son's closet, and the protective bubble he'd encased his thoughts in suddenly popped. Children drew on walls naturally, and Alex had been disciplined before for the graffiti he'd added to the décor of the living and dining rooms downstairs. Secretly, Franklin had been amused. He couldn't help but smile while working at his own desk, looking down to see his boy with his crayons and washable markers, propped up on his elbows, and drawing, drawing, drawing. The two of them filling empty page after empty page.

But the boy apparently wanted a larger canvas to work on. After being censured from the "public spaces" in the house, his response had been to take his art "underground", so to speak. In Alex's adolescence, the back of the closet would have been the hiding place for *Playboys* and sandwich baggies of weed. Right now, however, a mural that could be hanging in a gallery covered every inch of the back wall. In the space of about five feet, the art went from scribbles through a dalliance with Realism, and then headlong into Van Gogh and Munch. A teacher with a head like a hot-air balloon loomed over a classroom. A giant, flaming-eyed Hound of the Baskervilles—not unlike the chocolate Labrador from the next block over—prowled by the floorboards. A child's view of a world too tall and too large to hold in young hands. But the crayon had proved a magic wand cast over the giants of Life to shrink and shape them into things more manageable.

As he knelt, Franklin felt the nubs of half-a-dozen crayons bite at his knees. He scooped them up into his pocket on reflex as he stared at the drawings. Crude, yes. A technique not yet finding itself, but therein lay its power. This was so much more than a child's attempts to imitate reality. An imagination in communion with the inner souls of everyday objects was at work. Franklin poured over every image, examining every crayon stroke and every fleck of color where the wax did or did not hold to the surface of the wall. He followed the lines of every shape until he reached the far corner. At first glance, he thought that Alex had used the corner as a natural vanishing point of perspective—the crease in the wall made into a vertical horizon. Here the strokes were darker, denser. The dynamic motion of the whole street scene made it look like some of the buildings had been pulled into the angle of the walls— crushed and flattened as if sucked through a black hole.

How the hell did he do that? Franklin wondered.

He caught himself leaning forward. At first, he thought the visual effect was making him imagine a pull, like a magnet grabbing metal. He shifted his weight backwards to regain his balance, but didn't move. The air itself had closed around both his hands. A flash of panic collided with disbelief. The sensation spread up his arms and just as he thought he would topple backwards, Franklin suddenly pitched forward. He winced in anticipation of his face hitting the wall, but there was nothing there. A sound like rushing water filled his ears. Denial was no longer an option—he was caught and being dragged into the drawing. The air itself thickened and tightened over his face almost as close as his own skin. His last breath was trapped in his lungs, burning for release even as his chest demanded new air. Darkness crept into the corners of his vision, like a lamp slowly losing its glow. He felt like he was falling…

…falling…

…bones crushing…heat washing over…mind melting like butter in a saucepan, running in all directions at once in slow-motion…cannot hold the edges from the center…cannot hold the center…cannot hold…

A sudden jolt snapped Franklin awake. For a moment, his senses told him he was still whistling through the air and about to land hard, even though his body had already completed that action. He curled up to brace himself, and in the moment after, realized that it was the first independent motion he could remember performing since being back in his son's bedroom closet. A torrent of sensations flooded through him—the burning, the freezing, the choking. He took a huge intake of air and let it all out again in a primal scream.

When the last echo finally distanced and died, he rubbed his eyes. A milky-white fog crawled through the air around him. He thought for a minute that, somehow, in the act of falling, he'd actually risen into the clouds. *I should look for my wings*, he thought. Except that his body hurt too much for him to be dead. Every muscle screamed in complaint as Franklin worked to get to his feet, and the effort made his head swim. Even after he straightened, he couldn't quite tell if he were standing or floating.

Oh God, I've hit my head.

That one thought rang back and forth in his mind until he finally gave up waiting for it to explain what he was feeling. Franklin stared at the fog, watching to see if there was any pattern or sense of direction to the way that it flowed. At first, there wasn't any, but the longer he watched, the more he began to notice places where the mist seemed thin. He concentrated on one of these spots, like trying to peer through a blanket of gauze stretched to a point just shy of tearing. On the other side, he thought he could see shapes. None of them distinct—they were all a uniform gray-green that made it impossible to tell where the outline of one object might end and the next begin.

But then…something tickled the back of his mind. Some intuitive sense that he was looking at something familiar. He tried to hush his conscious mind, mute his clamorous thoughts about Alex, the mist, the drawings in the closet, and let that tiny voice from the furthest corner of his mind have all the attention.

He waited…

He waited…

…and somehow found himself remembering an old recliner—his favorite fall-asleep-watching-TV chair. Janice had been out to get rid of it from the first day they'd moved in together, and Franklin finally gave in just before Alex was born. The new living room furniture was all quite nice, but he still missed his favorite chair. It even used to sit in the perfect spot, just inside —

Suddenly Franklin's conscious and subconscious minds clicked together. *That's what I'm looking at!* he realized. On the other side of the fog was the corner of his living room, next to the doorway connecting the center hallway and opposite where the flatscreen TV used to hang on the wall. He had fallen from Alex's bedroom and landed in his own living room! And yet…not his living room.

Or perhaps it was he who was "not." Except the ache in his chest was very real, as was the thumping in his temples. Never in a dream had pain been so real, which meant that he was still "real." But standing on the other side of…

Yeah, he asked himself. *Standing on the other side of…what?*

As the questions piled on top of themselves, the roar of his conscious mind drowned out whatever further insights his subconscious might have had. But at least he could see just enough now through the fog to find his way…and if he could figure out that much…

Alex. It was insanity to believe his side of the fog was a real place, and further to think that he could find his son here, yet a mad hope was better than none. And the place to start looking was where it began— upstairs, in the back of Alex's closet. He took a step, and the "ground" shifted under his feet. It felt rough like stone beneath him, but moved when he moved as if the "solid ground" floated on something like water. With each movement, each shift of his weight even, he had to find his balance again.

The stairs were a particular challenge. His own weight pushed the stairs down to almost ground level as he stepped on them. He could tell he was making progress, but only at an inch at a time. The walking was as hard as picking one's feet in and out of snow drifts, and so by the time he'd gone halfway up, he had to stop and catch his breath.

Suddenly a chill—like stepping into the path of an Arctic wind— wrapped its embrace around Franklin. He had a sense of something moving behind him, and he immediately froze. From the furthest reaches of his most ancient instincts came a warning. A predator had arrived. It was close, and coming up behind him. Franklin tried to hold perfectly still, even as his traitorous body shivered violently. He didn't need to see to know. The Stranger. The Monster from the back of the closet, under the stairs, or any of the other places children wisely know to dread.

Daring to turn his head, Franklin watched the thing float closer. His body leaned forward, pulled to the Stranger, while his mind wrestled for control against the power that had hooked him. His body had nothing to hold onto, no anchor against the tide. His arms actually ached to embrace the monster, to feel its long fingers open his skin with their touch and wash his body in his own blood. He could practically taste the coppery scent in the air.

It brushed past Franklin so close that his flesh tingled, but somehow, the creature did not see him, and continued on by until it reached the top of the stairs and disappeared as swiftly as it had come. Several long minutes passed before the fear finally released Franklin from its grasp. And when it did, he collapsed—still too frightened to laugh from relief, too relieved to cry, and too beaten to stand. Death had practically walked straight up to him. He felt it come as near as a yawning chasm in his own chest waiting to swallow him. And some portion of his mind, somehow standing at a distance, told him it was because he had wanted it to come.

So why had he frozen? Tears began to stream from his eyes (*if only Janice could see!*). They rushed up and out of him like a rain-swollen river leaping its banks. If Alex was really here, on this side of reality, then the Stranger must have gotten him by now. And the only good left for Franklin to do was give himself to the creature too, but he was too selfish to die. Too vain, too self-absorbed even here in his dream between dreams. He wept his real tears in this unreal place, feeling the wetness on his cheeks and tasting the salt in the corners of his lips. The tears fell in a puddle, then a pool, then a pond, all around him. And then he wept even more.

An hour ticked by. Maybe longer, he couldn't tell. He had poured himself inside-out. His limbs weighed a ton; he couldn't raise his head even if he wanted to. All was as still as the grave inside his mind and his soul. In the silence, Franklin could hear the swirling fog cascading in the air. He could hear his heart pounding in his ears—hollow and distant.

...thump...thump...

If he'd been able to slip under the notice of the Stranger, then Alex could've too. His boy was clever. Clever enough to live. Franklin closed his eyes, and almost immediately memories he'd banished began to appear. Swim classes at the YMCA. Failing to convince Alex that he didn't need the training wheels on his bike any more—then the beaming joy when the boy discovered that fact on his own. The gnawing emptiness of the first day of school, and the thrilling rush at the sound of the school bus stopping at their corner.

His heart beat louder now...*thump...thump*. A tinny sound with a slight echo.

…thump…thump…thump…

Franklin looked up. That was not the sound of his own heart—this came from somewhere outside of him. He was on his feet before he even realized that he had strength in his limbs again, turning like a human antenna trying to pull in the best reception. The fog parted for him as he walked (or floated, it was hard to tell the difference) toward the sound. Upstairs? No—from the back of the house. The thumping beckoned to him and he opened himself to it, allowing it inside. *Not mine*, he reminded himself, but one in tight harmony with his own.

As he walked through what seemed to him to be the middle of his house—living room to dining room to kitchen—shapes began to appear, pale against the mist as if etched in white against a white background. They danced up to the edge of coming into focus, then melted away again. Franklin thought for a moment that he might be moving in circles, or maybe not at all. But any one of the thousands of memories of his son would not let him remain still. On and on, he walked.

There. Franklin's breath suddenly caught in his throat. The fog parted off to his left, as if blown aside by a phantom wind to reveal a figure in white. He glimpsed a face—only a glimpse, but he didn't need more. It couldn't be anyone but her. He turned in Janice's direction. He saw her five feet ahead of him, and then thirty, and then just out of arm's reach, and then far away again. Three months ago, she'd walked out of their house and he'd had nothing to say. *Three months?* he thought. A lifetime. And not a minute of it had passed without wanting to see her again. Maybe, with a second chance, he would know what to say.

…thump…thump… The sound grew louder, giving Franklin hope that he was actually crossing a distance even as Janice remained constantly out of reach. *Not Janice*, he thought. He wanted his wife, and the mist had sculpted something with a Janice-mask for him. Nevertheless, she appeared as a constant amidst the nothingness. He could focus on her, on where her green eyes were supposed to be, and hold his course.

Thump…Thump…

He stopped. At some point, without Franklin's awareness, the fog had thickened to his left and right to create a corridor between him and his wife. Had he passed through to outside of the house? He didn't know where he was now, where this place was supposed to be. What he could see for certain was Janice standing against the fog behind her—actually standing in it as if in bas-relief. Franklin took a step closer. She did not retreat.

THUMP…THUMP…THUMP…

Something stepped out of Janice, as if appearing out of her shadow, and began stretching higher and higher into the mist.

"Alex?"

The sound of his son's name almost didn't escape Franklin's lips. It seemed too heavy, too weighty a word for him to say. He looked up to see his son now tall enough to look through his own bedroom window from the backyard. Alex's face appeared like the moon amidst the clouds, hanging low and full just above the treetops. The boy's eyes and mouth and soft smile were so much like his own, and yet simpler. Uninformed by time and unpracticed in the adult art of masking thoughts and meaning. Franklin saw himself—wiped clean and reset back to the beginning of himself.

A ball dropped from Alex's hands—the size of a recliner when it first appeared, then shrinking as it fell to a more normal size. It hit the "ground" and started bouncing toward Franklin. *thump…thump…* Slow. *thump…thump…* Slow and steady.

Just before it reached him, the ball took a high hop and hung in the air just out of reach. Time held its breath. *Play catch, Dad! Play catch!* A warmth flooded through Franklin, as if his blood had begun to run for the first time. From inside his chest, the sunlight of a most simple, perfect joy made the mist around him begin to glow. He caught Alex's ball, and in that instant, thick shadows fell across the fog. The light turned hard and cold, and the mist suddenly rolled as if a terrible wind had blown through. Alex and Janice began to turn away and started to disappear as if around a corner. Alarms blared in Franklin's head. He glanced over his shoulder, sensing what he would see before his eyes registered it. A darkness filling the fog behind him and in its midst, The Stranger. His skin was a sharp-white, eyes like a shark's. He glided closer, slender arms dangling at his sides, fingers scraping together and making a sound like knives being sharpened.

Franklin dropped the ball and lumbered toward where Alex and Janice had gone, his body suddenly thick and heavy. He found a turn in the corridor there, and another hallway with his family running ahead of him. Janice jerked stiffly as if most of her joints were like stone. Franklin quickly caught up to her, took her by the hand, and they chased after their son together. The hallway felt as if it were grading uphill, slowing them down.

Franklin pushed Janice ahead of him and tried to send her on with a warning, but his own voice came out no louder than a whisper. Close at his heels and ahead of the Stranger, the darkness was consuming the mist like water being pulled down a drain. The solid footing under Franklin's feet melted like wax, and he could feel himself sinking to his ankles, to his knees, and up to his thighs. A strong current grabbed at his legs, trying to pull him back towards the darkness.

His mind screamed orders that his body was slow to obey. Franklin lifted his legs up and out of the fog as best he could, but he was trying to go uphill and up-current at the same time. The corridor of fog was re-casting itself into a gulley, and the sides became steeper with every passing minute. It was a race to the rim to escape the pull into the bottom below and the clutch of the Stranger.

He heard a scream from above, and the angle of the climb pitched suddenly sharper. Franklin looked up to see Janice hurtling towards him in a free-fall. He felt himself start to slide, and then a massive fist closed around his left hand. Alex had grabbed hold of him—and in the same instant, Franklin reached out and caught Janice's hand just as she fell past. Her momentum nearly popped his arm out of its socket, but he somehow held. They all held—hand-to-hand like links in a chain, dangling over death.

But they were still slipping—slowly and certainly—toward the bottom. Franklin felt Alex's grip on him like a vise, but his hold on Janice was far more tenuous. She was dead weight hanging on the end of his arm, and the rushing current pulled and pushed on her from top to bottom. His arm was like rubber—all the strength in his muscles had been spent just to catch her—and now, like an anchor, she was dragging all three of them to the bottom.

He glanced back over his shoulder at Alex, into those innocent eyes. Time to make a decision. *No, more than that,* Franklin thought. *Time to act on a decision.* By the time he turned back, it was as if what he'd chosen had already begun. Cracks ran across the face of the Janice-mask and began to bleed. Her body trembled, caught in her own personal quake while a rumble like thunder rolled up from below.

Franklin let go. The flow of gravity and the current seemed to reverse themselves, and he and Alex shot up and over the rim. There was a roaring sound behind them, and suddenly a geyser of hot ash. It blew past Franklin, scalding him head to foot. He looked around, and his mouth went dry. The mist was stained with blood, soaking into the rolling gray clouds and filling the air with a hot, metallic scent.

The solid footing under him began to shift again. Franklin retreated from the expanding hole until he met resistance against his back. The fog had hardened here on three sides, creating a pocket. Alex fell to a sitting position, with Franklin standing between his knees. The darkness opened for them still, unsatisfied and unsated. From within, Franklin could sense its utter emptiness. A void of thought, feeling, all being. He thought of Janice, but she was like a blank page in a book to him now. He had a vague recollection that something was supposed to be there, but no idea what.

He reached into his pocket and found the crayon nubs. One orange one was still big enough for him to manipulate, and he knelt to experiment with drawing a line in the mist on the "ground" in front of him. The color held even against the darkening background. Quickly, he began to sketch. Several lines meeting at a common point, the other ends pulled and foreshortened along the edges.

Alex bent over to look at what his father was doing. "Daddy?"

Franklin didn't answer, didn't take the time to say that he had nothing to say. He blended the shadings, feeling the crayon start to disintegrate in his hands. *My son could do this,* Franklin thought. He kept working until he started to feel a tug, a new current, pulling at his fingertips.

"Where does this one go, Daddy?" Alex asked.

Franklin grabbed him by the hand (by the finger, actually) and pulled him to the edge.

"Where does this one go?" the boy asked again.

About the Author

S. R. Dixon's short stories have appeared in more than a dozen print and online magazines devoted to horror and dark fantasy, including *Night Terrors*, *City Slab*, *MOOREEFFOC Magazine*, and *Black Petals*. As a playwright, his full-length titles include *The Nutcracker & The Mouse King*, adapted from the original E.T.A. Hoffmann novella, and *A Midnight Dreary*, about the life of Edgar Allan Poe. He is a member of The Playwrights' Center and The Dramatists Guild of America.

For employment, Scott has held most of the traditional starving-artist jobs at one time or another: substitute teacher, waiter, bartender, mobile DJ. Since 2003, he's been a resident artist with The Commonweal Theatre Company in Lanesboro, Minnesota, where he's appeared on stage in more than thirty productions to date. His greatest claim to fame, however, is from playing the brilliant (but mad!) Dr. Smirnoff in the film *Mutant Swinger from Mars* from DarkArt Entertainment.

About the Editor

Nicholas Ozment co-edited *MOOREEFFOC Magazine* (2000-2002) and currently co-edits *Every Day Poets* (everydaypoets.com). He also co-edited the first EDP anthology, *Best of Every Day Poets* (Every Day Publishing 2010). He received his M.A. in English Literature and Language from WSU, where he teaches English composition and literature.

His own stories, poems, essays, and reviews span a wide range of genres and styles, and his award-winning work has been anthologized, podcast, and performed on stage and radio. Recently his flash fiction was anthologized in *The Best of Every Day Fiction Two* (Every Day Publishing 2010) and *Through Blood and Iron* (Ricasso Press 2010) and his whimsical illustrated fantasy, *Knight Terrors: The (Mis)Adventures of Smoke the Dragon*, will be released fall 2010 by Cyberwizard Productions.

He lives in Minnesota with his wife and daughter.

6254133R0

Made in the USA
Charleston, SC
03 October 2010